Maggie & Abby's NEVERENDING PILLOW FORT

Maggie & Abby's NEVERENDING PILLOW FORT

WILL TAYLOR

HARPER

An Imprint of HarperCollinsPublishers

ISBN 978-0-06-264431-2

Typography by Jessie Gang
18 19 20 21 22 CG/LSCH 10 9 8 7 6 5 4 3 2 1
❖

For my mom

ONE

There's no sound in the world quite like the sound of a cat getting stuck to an ice cream truck.

Most kids would have missed it. But after six weeks without Abby, six weeks of being almost completely on my own, six weeks where going out to get the mail was becoming the best part of my day, my senses were on high alert for anything even halfway interesting while I was out there.

It went down blink by blink. In perfect. Slow. Motion.

Plink-plink-doop-doodle-doo-plink! went the ice cream truck parked innocently across the street, its music filling the summer afternoon.

Mrreow! went Samson, Abby's huge black-and-white cat, launching himself at something small and buzzy near the back of the truck.

Kschkt! went Samson's snagglepaw, the one with the claws he couldn't pull back, latching with a plasticky crinkle onto the vinyl banner advertising Robo Pops and Chocolate Swirl Bars and Fun-Fun Rainbow Crispys.

Slam! went Caitlin, the high school senior across the street, who always stopped to use her own bathroom when she was out on her ice cream route, leaving her house with her eyes glued to her phone.

Mrreow! went Samson again, tugging forlornly at his paw. The banner shook, but the cat stayed stuck.

Caitlin was laughing at something happening on her screen. She didn't see Samson. She climbed into the driver's seat. She turned on the engine.

Hey, no, wait! went my heart.

If Caitlin drove away, Samson could get hurt. He could lose his claws for good.

Or worse, Caitlin might back up and Samson could be killed.

Or Caitlin might start driving, see Samson in her side mirror, panic-drive into a utility pole, and then *Caitlin* could be killed.

Or she might slam on the brakes, making a truck that could possibly be behind her by then veer out of the way to avoid her, jump the curb, and hit me instead, and then *I* could be killed.

Or a truck could be coming from one way and a school bus from the other, and Caitlin might still be laughing at her phone, and in the confusion *all* of us could be killed.

This was a potential disaster on an epic scale. This was the *Titanic* pulling away with every kitten on Earth napping in the cargo hold. No! This was the space shuttle counting down to liftoff with an entire kindergarten class hiding under its booster rockets!

I had to do something. Options, Maggie, options . . .

Got it. Get the shuttle operator's attention.

"Caitlin!" I yelled.

No response. My call was lost in the plinking roar of the musical liftoff engines. I stepped forward to cross the spaceport tarmac, but a lunar cargo supply truck zoomed by from the other direction and I flinched back. I couldn't get out there in time—it was too dangerous.

Mrreow! cried the cornered kindergarten class. Through the waffle cone decals on the shuttle window I saw the pilot strap herself in and snap her visor down. I had seconds to act.

I stared around desperately, then looked down at my hands and smiled. They were full of flares, charged and ready for use. Of course! I'd planned for this! I always planned ahead, because something could always go wrong.

I planted my feet right on the edge of the tarmac, took a

deep breath, threw both hands up and out and forward, and shouted again, giving it everything I'd got just as the shuttle began to move.

"Hey!" My voice rang around the space depot, echoing off the shining chrome buildings, rising to a roar as the flares exploded into thousands of shining white sparks flying through the air in all directions. The wind blew my hair back, and I laughed in triumph and relief as the driver looked up and the shuttle slammed to a halt.

The fire in its engine died.

"Hey," Caitlin called, rolling down her window. "You dropped your mail."

I blinked and looked around. She was right. The mail I'd just collected was scattered on the hot street between us: five or six envelopes and a catalog for discount wrapping paper.

"You caught a cat," I said, pointing. Caitlin quirked an eyebrow. I looked both ways and jogged across the road. Caitlin turned off the engine and got out.

"Oh, hey," she said as I unhooked Samson from her truck. "That's not good at all." She scratched Samson's ears. "Sorry I almost dragged you off, buddy. Lucky you were out here to see him, Maggie."

Luck had nothing to do with it, I thought. *A special agent–rescue specialist trained in the use of flares always knows where and when she'll be needed.*

The wind blew through my hair.

"Sure," I said, gathering Samson up into my arms. He was already purring. "Thanks for stopping."

Caitlin laughed. "Like I had a choice. I've seen people do a lot of weird things to flag down an ice cream truck, but no one's ever thrown their mail at me before."

I looked up and down the street. There were no cars coming, but if I didn't get the remains of those flares picked up quick, I'd have to explain to my mom why her catalog had tire tracks on it. "Hey, do you think . . . ?" I said, shrugging Samson to show that my hands were full.

"Course," said Caitlin. "You saved the day."

I repeated that phrase to myself, picturing a glorious victory parade for me going down our street as Caitlin gathered the mail and tucked it under my arm.

"Was this yours too?" she asked, holding up a cheap plastic pen. I squinted at it. Ah, yes, the hypno-raygun I'd been flipping through my fingers when I approached the mailbox. You never know when those things will come in handy.

"You keep it," I said generously. "I've got plenty more."

"Um, okay, thanks." Caitlin slipped the pen into her pocket. "Here, hang on a second." She opened the back of the truck and rummaged around, emerging with a wrapped Mega Ultra Caramel Swizzle Cone. "On me," she said, setting it in my elbow beside Samson.

"Wow, thanks! I mean"—I dropped my voice, trying to be cool and not sound like, I don't know, a third grader—"you don't have to do that."

"You helped me out." Caitlin shrugged. "And you've been alone a whole lot this summer. Thought maybe you could use a pick-me-up or something."

"Huh?" I said. "How do you know I've been alone?"

Caitlin pulled out her phone again. "I live across the street, remember? I see you all the time sitting up on your roof, or staring into space every time you get the mail. Your friend went to summer camp without you, right?"

"Abby? Yeah, she went to camp." This was weird. So Caitlin had been watching me, had she? I began assessing which rival spy agency she might be working for. "How did you . . . ?"

"You've got a postcard from her in there." Caitlin nodded toward the mail getting sweaty in my armpit. "Plus one of her brothers told me." She tilted her head toward the turquoise house one to the right of mine. Abby's house. Her twin brothers had stayed home all summer. I'd seen them playing soccer in their front yard. But they were juniors in high school and about as likely to hang out with a soon-to-be-sixth grader like me as Caitlin was.

"Abby's coming home soon though," I said. "Very soon."

Suddenly I was burning with impatience. My arms were

full of successfully rescued cat, free ice cream, and, apparently, the latest postcard from Abby. This mission was officially over. "Anyway, thanks again for the Swizzle Cone," I said, scanning the road.

"Sure, sure. Thanks for saving me from the cat, or the other way around. Hope your summer gets better," Caitlin said, tapping at her phone. Then she stopped and looked up at me. Really looked. "You know what?" she said. "I'm sorry. I shouldn't have assumed just because you're alone you're not okay. People can have amazing things going on in their lives that no one else knows about. I bet you're having a whole summer full of awesome adventures, aren't you?" She smiled, patting me on the shoulder. "Of course you are. You go get 'em, tiger!" And she returned to the truck.

It was my turn to quirk an eyebrow. Yeah, definitely not suspicious behavior. Definitely not clearly working for a counterspy agency....

I got out a hurried "You too!" as Caitlin closed the door; then I crossed back to my own territory. The tinkling of the ice cream truck faded in the distance as Samson twisted lazily out of my arms and dropped onto the grass, taking the mail and ice cream with him.

"You're welcome, buddy," I called as his tail disappeared through the gap in the fence leading to Abby's place. I wiped my forehead. I loved that cat, but hypno-rayguns, he was heavy.

My house phone jangled through the open kitchen window as I scooped up the ice cream and letters, and I hustled in to answer it.

"Hi, Mom," I said, hopping up on the counter. I tucked the phone against my neck and started flipping through the mail. Bill. Bill. Junk. Bill. Junk. Catalog. Hey, a second postcard!

"Hi, sweetie. How's the day?"

"Fine. I rescued Abby's cat from a killer ice cream truck, and I just got another postcard from Uncle Joe."

"Aw. I should probably be mad my little brother writes to you more than me." The intercom buzz and bustle of the hospital break room echoed behind her. "How's he doing?"

I scanned the postcard. "Good. Same as the last few months: Alaska, whales, cabin, whales, research, sciency science. Aaand more whales!"

"That's Joe. What's that crinkling noise I'm hearing?"

"That is the sound of a Mega Ultra Caramel Swizzle Cone being unwrapped," I said. "Caitlin across the street gave it to me."

"That was nice of her. I'm glad you're spending time with other people. Make sure you eat something with vegetables for dinner, though."

I just barely avoided a sigh. "You won't be home?"

"—be right there," my mom said to someone who wasn't me. "What, sweetie? No, that's why I called. I'll be working late again."

"I'm shocked," I said, biting off a chunk of ice cream.

"Oh, don't start," said my mom. "Deep, slow breath, you'll be fine. Hang on— *No, I said I'll be right there. Well, I think Philips should be able to handle that without me by now. One second—* Sweetie, sorry, but I really have to go. Remember what I said about dinner, and make sure you get your chores done, okay?"

I took another bite. I was powering my way through that ice cream. "Yes, Mom," I said around a mouthful of caramel crunchy bits. And really, what else was there to say? I'd been used to my mom being gone since she got promoted to head doctor in the kids-with-cancer ward. And now that I was eleven-staring-down-twelve and she trusted me to be okay on my own all day, I was starting to forget what she looked like.

I was fine with it before, when I had school stuff and Abby was around, but things hadn't gone to plan this summer, and after six long weeks of being really, truly, actually alone—if you don't count those first two weeks of oh-my-ice-cream-let's-not-talk-about-it beginner tennis lessons, which went about as well as me around a group of strange new kids has ever gone—I could say for certain it wasn't much fun at all.

"Okay then, real good-bye now," said my mom. "Love you. See you soon."

"You too," I replied. My mom hung up first.

Well hey, another night of being all by my lonesome. I stuffed the last of the ice cream into my mouth, fished Abby's postcard out of the bill pile, and headed for my pillow fort in the living room.

The fort's technical name was Gromit's Room, after Abby's favorite movie, but with no Abby around to get the inside joke I'd just been calling it my Fortress of Fortitude. At least it was cool and comfortable after my cat-carrying marathon in the afternoon heat. I flicked on the lamp, re-armed myself with a new pen from the arts-and-crafts corner, and settled back against the sofa cushions to read the latest from Camp Cantaloupe.

Maggles! I saw a turtle today. I named it Brandon McPondy. It pooped beside the lake. Wish you were here! Can't believe it's almost over! Home Thursday!

Abs

That was all.

Only. Wait. Wait wait wait-wait-wait. Thursday. TODAY Thursday?!

I sat up, staring around as though some total stranger would appear and confirm that yes, today was the fifth day of the week and this glorious news was true. I punched the air, my mood doing a complete one eighty.

Abby was coming home today!

But there was something weird going on with the post-card. This was Abby's very last message, so why was she still writing in code? She'd been sending cheerfully pointless cards every other day since she got to camp, all way too out of character to be anything but secret messages, but for the life of me I'd never been able to work out what her encryption system was. I'd been counting on some sort of big reveal at the end, but here she was keeping the act going right up to the final card. It was very mysterious. Camp Cantaloupe must have been such a horrible, oppressive place that she couldn't risk saying any more until she was safely home.

Of course, Camp Cantaloupe wouldn't have been horrible if I'd been able to go with her like we'd planned. Then it would have been, like Abby said, ah-may-zing. Then instead of waking up week after week to a silent house and boring chores, I'd have been waking up to a log cabin with splintery floors, dead wasps in the windows, and Abby snoring away in the bunk below me. And when we lined up for roll call, we would have been standing side by side because our last names are close, and they would call out *"Hernandez, Abigail!"* and Abby would shout *"Hair!"* and I would smile, and they would call *"Hetzger, Margaret!"* and I would shout *"Peasant!"* and Abby would snort. And then we'd steal all the red and orange Froot Loops from the mess hall and the games would really begin. Camp Cantaloupe would never know what hit it.

But we didn't go to camp together. Our plans failed. And all because my overworked mom forgot to send in my camp registration paperwork, and by the time anyone realized, it was too late. Abby did everything she could to cancel, but we couldn't stop it: we were doomed to spend the first half of our last summer before sixth grade and middle school—where, if the stories were true, everything was going to change and the earth's crust would break into pieces and the world as we'd known it would be turned upside down—horribly, tragically apart.

I reread Abby's card, looking for hidden patterns. *"Can't believe it's almost over."* What could that mean? Abby had promised she would hate every minute of camp without me, and these messages—all on official, silly Camp Cantaloupe postcards—were so Fun-Fun Rainbow Crispy cheerful they *had* to be fake. My co–secret agent just did not use that many exclamation marks.

And what about the other clues? Along with her steady stream of postcards, Abby had sent back a map of the campgrounds, a speckled owl feather, and a scarf she'd made out of an old patchwork quilt during her first arts-and-crafts lesson. I'd spent a whole week working out rescue missions based on the map, but had to give it up when I realized none of them were really doable without my own helicopter. The scarf and feather became Abby-themed decorations in my fort, but what if all those things were actually a cunning key to decode the postcards, and I'd somehow missed it? Me, the world's greatest secret agent? I'd never live it down.

I glanced at the picture on the front of the card, which showed Orcas Island and, for some reason, a goofy-looking moose, and shoved it in the very back of my postcard shoe box alongside all the others. That was it, then. It was over. My best friend was coming home, and one way or another I was finally going to get the answers to all my questions.

Nothing to do now but climb up on the roof and wait.

It got pretty hot sometimes, but every day that summer I'd braved the heat and the danger and clambered up roof-side, staring out west past Seattle and Puget Sound toward Orcas Island. Somewhere out there, somewhere past that darn pine tree blocking my view, Abby was trapped all alone at camp, waiting, counting down the days just like I was.

Which meant we were waiting together.

Only, as the scorching July days dragged by, I'd had to admit I was starting to feel, despite all my training and patience, maybe just the teeniest bit . . . lonely.

* * *

Which might explain why I screamed like a third grader presented with pie when the Hernandezes' car crunched into the driveway next door with a back seat full of duffel bags and a front seat full of . . . Abby!

I scrambled off the roof so fast I almost broke my neck. We met in the middle of Abby's lawn and slammed our arms around each other.

"Abs!"

"Maggles!"

We hug-danced around and around and around. We stepped back.

Abby looked fantastic. She had a hearty sunburn, impressive scratches on her arms, and a fancy new side braid in her dark, curly hair. She was also taller than me somehow. I squinted. She actually looked pretty different. She looked like . . . New Abby.

Wait, I thought, for the first time all summer, *what do I look like? Am I New Maggie?* I felt the same, and I knew from the mirror that morning that I still had my usual choppy bangs, square jaw, and independent eyebrows. Abby was smiling, though, so I must have been doing okay.

"Look at you!" she said, bopping me on the arm. "Look at your tan. I missed you."

"You too," I said, bopping her back. "And how dare you get taller without me?"

"Did I?" Abby stood up straighter. "It must have been all the tree climbing. And swimming. And hiking and every-thing and—" She grabbed my arm. "Mags, summer camp is the best thing everrrrrr!"

Wait. What?

"Oh, come on, you can drop the act," I said. "You're safe now. What was your code, anyhow? You better tell me right this second. I've been trying to crack it all summer."

It was Abby's turn to blink. "Code? What code?"

"The coded messages. In your postcards."

"I never sent any coded messages in my postcards."

We stared at each other. Something wasn't adding up here. "But . . . you did," I said. "Remember? All that *I love camp and stargazing-in-the-canoe out on the sparkly perfect lake* talk, and everything."

"Well yeah, I wrote that 'cause I did love it. Obviously."

The pieces of the summer puzzle I thought I was working on split apart and began swirling around in my brain, form-ing new, awkward shapes. "But . . . when you left you said you wouldn't," I said. "You promised to hate it."

"Yeah, but I didn't understand about camp back then," said Abby, shrugging. She made it sound like a lifetime ago. "When I got there it turned out to be ah-may-zing!"

The sun was beating down on my shoulders, and Abby was right there in front of me, but for a moment I wondered if any of this was really happening. Maybe I'd fallen off the roof and hit my head after all. That would explain the spinning sensation in my stomach.

"But Abs, I really thought you were miserable," I said. "I spent the whole first month planning out rescue missions to get you back."

"Ha! That's right," said Abby. "You said in your letters. I'm glad you kept busy playing your games. I was kinda worried about you being all on your own here, to be honest."

Wait, wait, wait. *My* games? Hidden hideouts and secret codes and daring island rescues were *our* games. And why on earth had she been worried about me? I was the one safe at home where I belonged.

Abby heaved an arm around my shoulders and squeezed. "Seriously, Mags, I have so many stories to tell you. But first you have to tell me all about your summer. Oh! And where's this fort-base thing you built?"

I hitched on a smile, determined to keep my cool. It was hard considering I felt like the ground was crumbling away beneath my feet, but I managed it.

"Come on, I'll show you," I said. "How'd you, uh, get all those scratches, by the way?"

"Oh, one of the older girls tried to bully me by throwing my backpack in the blackberry brambles."

"Did you get it back?"

"Yup," said Abby, with a grin I'd never seen on her sweet face before. "I might have left hers in there instead, though."

She followed me into the living room, where my glorious fort took up most of the floor.

"Whoa!" Abby stopped dead. "This is awesome! How does your mom feel about it?"

I shrugged. At first my mom had been really unhappy about having her living room torn up, but after a few pointed comments from me about how it wouldn't have happened if I'd been away at camp like we'd planned, she let me get on with it. I felt a little bad about making her feel guilty—she was super busy taking care of sick kids, after all—but not bad enough to give up my Fortress of Fortitude.

"Ooo!" Abby said, crawling in. "I love it. It's so you."

I looked around, trying to figure out what was *me* about it. It was a big fort—I'd definitely been ambitious—but other than that it looked like any one of my typical brilliant, well-organized secret lairs. One thing I've learned over the years: if you're going to be taking part in epic adventures ranging from international spy agency wars to intergalactic dinosaur smuggling, it helps to start with a neat base.

"Aw, hey!" Abby said, reaching up and batting at the patchwork scarf hanging from the ceiling. "I made you this."

"I know. I love it. And here, uh, somewhere . . ." I dug

around in the arts-and-crafts corner and pulled out a bundle. "I made you this."

Abby opened it. "A scarf! You made me a denim scarf. With gold tassels!"

"Old jeans and curtains. Sorry, I didn't have any patchwork quilts to work with."

"That's okay. I wouldn't have either without the craft bin at Camp Cantaloupe," said Abby. "It's crammed with all the things campers have left behind over the years. I found the quilt right at the bottom. But I love this scarf so much!"

She put the scarf around her neck—it looked ridiculous—and grabbed me in another hug. Hello, New Abby. Old Abby never hugged this much. She even smelled different, like woodsmoke and fruit punch and coconut sunscreen. My heart gave a pang.

"Oh, it is so, *so* good to see you," she said, letting me go. "But why did we make each other scarves? It's eighty-five degrees outside."

"You started it."

"That's all they taught us how to sew before we moved on to candle making."

"Whee. Sounds fun."

"Ha!" Abby adjusted her scarf and leaned back against the sofa. She looked even older in the lamplight. "It was, actually. You have to promise me you'll absolutely, seriously go next year. No matter what. I don't even know how I'm going to wait that long. Camp Cantaloupe"—she raised her hands toward the ceiling—"is the beeeesssssstt!"

My stomach lurched. This wasn't cool. If there really had been no secret codes coming in from Abby, and no messages hidden in the presents she'd sent me, then that meant I'd wasted the whole first half of summer trying to figure it all out for nothing. That meant Abby really *had* had a wonderful six weeks without me. That meant I really had been alone. And that meant we needed to start the summer over, right here, right now.

It was time to put this camp business behind us.

"Yeah," I pointed out, "you already said. But you're home now! And I have the most amazing idea for a new game. It's based around this place, which is actually called, wait for it, Gromit's Room! Now, I know you don't need me to explain the name, but I thought—"

"Let's play something else," said Abby, flipping through the books stacked along one wall. I stopped, my mouth hanging open. "Something with more people," Abby went on. "I've gotten really used to having lots of people around. Or at least let's do something more— OH!" Her head snapped up. "We can do camp! We can start a summer camp game!"

I stared at her. "But you're finally back from camp. . . ."

"And this way I don't have to be! I'll teach you all the

songs and the official camp dance and we can find other kids to join and yes! Project!" She was using even more exclamation marks than she had in her postcards. She whapped me with the tassels on her scarf. "So, this fort or cave or whatever will be your cabin now, yeah? That means it needs a real cabin name. What do you want to call it?"

Oof. Abby was moving way too fast. Way too fast without me, and I'd only just gotten her back. *If I have gotten her back*, said a suspicious voice in my head. Maybe this New Abby was some sort of robot clone. Was that a hidden seam running along the side of her jaw . . . ? No, no, I couldn't start thinking that way. Old Abby was under there somewhere. It just might take a little time to bring her all the way home.

And hey, at least she was enthusiastic. I could play along for now, and we could start the summer over with Abby's camp theme, and once things got rolling I'd be able to step in and take the reins just like always.

"Um, I dunno. I guess I could call it Fort . . . Mc . . . Forterson?"

New Abby snorted. "Cute. Okay, then, let's go make my cabin-fort! It'll have to go in my bedroom, but I bet my dad will totally let us tear apart the sofa in the garage. And I can tell you all my camp stories while we build it!" She unfolded her extra-long limbs and stretched, knocking over one of the wall pillows and exposing the row of wooden chair legs behind it.

"Whoops!" she said, repairing the damage as the bed-sheet roof sagged alarmingly. "Sorry. Let's get out of here before I totally destroy your cabin. It's probably too early to have a supervillain wrecking your base and spoiling all your plans."

Ahh, that sounded like Old Abby.

"Does that mean you're volunteering when we need one?" I asked, reaching out and tweaking her fancy new braid.

Abby's eyes narrowed, and she grinned her new grin. "You'll just have to wait and see."

TWO

Loud pop music blared from the kitchen as we walked through Abby's back door, and the tightness in my chest eased as the familiar warm smells of the Hernandezes' place rolled over me.

"Dad," Abby called. "I brought Maggie over!" She turned to me. "Okay, seriously, it is so weird to be home."

Abby's dad bounded out of the kitchen, a giant bowl of corn and peppers balanced in one hand and a wooden spoon in the other.

"Maggie! So good to see you again!"

"Hey, Alex," I said. "You too." Alex and I were on first-name terms. He was Dad to Abby and her twin brothers, and Mr. Hernandez to his art students up at the high school, but he had always been Alex to me.

"I've spotted you perched majestically up on your roof a

few times this summer," Alex said, stirring wildly. "You were drenched in the light of the setting sun like a Pre-Raphaelite muse. Looked like fun! But aren't you just so incredibly glad to have Abby home?"

"Totally!"

"Of course you are. And did you hear how much she loved camp? I'm so glad she went. You *have* to go back with her next year. She can show you around and introduce you to all the other kids!" A burst of corn and pepper chunks escaped the bowl and scattered decoratively over the floor. "I put your bags in your room for you, by the way, Abby," Alex went on. "I knew you wouldn't want to waste one second before reuniting with your best friend."

"Thanks, Dad," said Abby. "Hey, can we take the cushions off the garage sofa and build a fort in my bedroom?"

"Sure! Sounds like an amazing project! Whatever you do, don't let me interfere. Can you stay for dinner, Maggie? We're having a feast in honor of Abby's homecoming."

"Absolutely, thanks," I said.

"Victory! I'd better get back in there, then." He danced into the kitchen, and loud singing started up a moment later.

I turned to Abby. "I think I missed your family more than I missed you," I said. She whapped me on the arm.

"Come on," she said. "Pillow time, and then I have *so* many camp stories to tell you."

We waded into the cheerful mess of Abby's house,

stepping past laundry baskets, stacks of books, construction-paper animal heads, newspapers, soccer blankets over mismatched chairs, cat toys, random shoes, and all the other comfortable clutter of a family that was actually, well, *home* most of the time.

"Did your brothers miss you?" I asked as we headed down the hall, but before Abby could answer, a teenage boy bounded out of a doorway to our left, followed by another, and she was lifted right off her feet.

"Hey, Matt! Who's this stranger wandering around our house?" said the first boy.

"Ooh, I don't know, Mark," said Matt, a perfect copy of his twin except for the bike accident scar curving down his cheek. "She looks a bit like that girl we used to know. What was her name . . . Abby? Only this girl's made of muscle and she's ten feet tall. Where's Abby, you burly stranger? What have you done with her?"

"It's me, you goons," said Abby, laughing as she fought her way free. I smiled. There was Old Abby.

"Hey, now here's someone we can trust," said Matt, spotting me. "Tell it to us straight, Maggie: Is this really our sister?"

"Yefinally," I said, ducking my head a little. All the blood in my entire body stampeded to my face. "I mean definitely! Totally. Yes."

Matt and Mark Hernandez were sixteen. They were tall. They played soccer and baseball and rode bikes and were very, very popular. And it was weird to say, seeing as I'd known them since forever, but they were getting to be seriously cute.

Especially, um, Matt.

"I guess it is you, then," Matt said, holding Abby at arm's length. "If Maggie says so then we'll let you pass."

"Do we get to hear all about your adventures at camp?" Mark asked, propping an elbow on his brother's shoulder. Gah, they were adorable.

"Obviously," said Abby, "at dinner. But right now Maggie and I have work to do."

"Work?" said Matt, stepping back.

"During summer vacation?" said Mark, putting a hand over his heart.

"Work," said Abby, her hands on her hips.

The twins screamed and dove back into their bedroom. Abby snorted, and we continued down the hall.

"Missed you!" called the twins.

"You too!" Abby called back.

In the Hernandezes' musty, jam-packed garage we stripped the cushions off the old orange-plaid sofa, then hauled them back to Abby's little bedroom.

"Ohhhh, there you are," she said, dropping her armful of

cushions in the doorway and throwing herself dramatically onto the bed. "Seriously, Mags," she rumbled into the comforter, "if there was one thing I missed at camp, it was my perfect, wonderful mattress." I coughed loudly. She looked up. "Oh, right. And you, I guess."

I threw a cushion at her.

With no bulky sofa to build around, we had to improvise a rougher pillow fort than mine, but after three or four collapses we managed to construct a lopsided dome in the corner between the foot of Abby's bed and her desk. It was super cozy, with just enough room for both of us to sit or one of us to stretch out, and once it was filled with pillows, blankets, sleeping bags, and Abby's old stuffed animals, it became a big squashy nest of comfortable.

For finishing touches Abby brought in a spare desk lamp with a bright-pink shade, I hung the denim-and-gold-tassel scarf across the ceiling to match the patchwork one in mine, Abby pinned a sign saying *Fort Comfy* over the entrance, and her pillow fort was done.

And I had to admit, it was pretty great. I hadn't planned on Abby having her own fort—that was supposed to be *my* thing—but this place could really come in handy once our games got going: spare food supply depot, cocoon for hatching Venomous Wolfbird eggs, emergency backup base in case our primary base got discovered by enemies or invaded by warrior jellyfish. There were so many options once Abby got tired of playing, ugh, summer camp.

"Okay," Abby said as we snuggled in. "This is so perfect. You've got your cabin, I've got my cabin, now we need a name for the camp itself. By our cabins combined, we are Camp ... Camp ... hmm ... Camp Bestie?"

"Really?" I said, although I couldn't help smiling. "Even I think that's silly. What if we combine our names: Camp Magabby? Camp Abbgie?"

"Ew, no. And I think the name should say more about what the camp is."

"Fine. Camp ... Spymaster, then?"

"This isn't that kind of camp, Mags. We're talking summer camp here. Maybe Camp Sofa Cabin?"

"What about Camp Pillow Pile? Or, oooh—!"

Abby sat up and our eyes locked.

"Camp Pillow Fort," we said together. And I had to admit I liked it.

"Obviously," said Abby. "Okay—" She glanced past my shoulder. "Hey! Samson, no!"

I turned to see my favorite cat in the world pushing through the brand-new entrance flap, a dead mouse clamped between his teeth.

"Aw, buddy," said Abby. "Get that out of here!"

Samson blinked adoringly at her, then gently laid the

mouse right on Creepy Frog, a gangly, googly-eyed stuffed monstrosity Abby had loved since forever.

I leaned in for a better look. "I think it's a welcome-home present. Isn't a mouse sort of like a dozen roses coming from a cat?"

"Yay, me," said Abby. She squeezed Samson and kissed the top of his head. "Thanks, I guess, buddy. I'm happy to see you, too, but there were plenty of mice in my last cabin and I don't want any in this one." She picked the mouse up by its tail and crawled out of the fort.

"Hi again," I said, grabbing Samson around the middle and burying my face in his fur. He nudged me briefly with his cheek, then slipped free and started exploring the new space, kneading happily through the piles of soft things. Well, half kneading, half getting stuck with his snagglepaw.

"All right," said Abby, poking her head back into the fort. "Mouse returned to the great outdoors. But now it's go time! I want to get this unpacking done before dinner."

So, for what was left of the afternoon, Abby unpacked, and Abby talked, and I listened, stretched out in the entrance to the fort with my chin in my hands, Samson purring beside me.

Abby told me every single detail about life at Camp Cantaloupe. She told me about her splintery, wasp-infested cabin, the terrible food—"Cucumber casserole is not a thing!"—the embarrassing sing-alongs, the goofy counselors, and the unbelievable summer stars. She told me about the kids who'd been going to camp for years already, and about the kids like her who were there for the first time. She told me about all her new friends.

And it was awful. Sure, I'd wanted to go to Camp Cantaloupe once too, but I hadn't; and there was only so long I could hear about things I'd never done, places I'd never seen, and kids I'd never met before I started to feel even more left behind than I had that morning.

So it came as a serious relief when we heard a loud knock and Alex's head appeared around the door.

"Hi, you two," he said, "dinner will be ready in— Ooo, hey! Nice fort!"

"Thanks, Dad.'"

"Why's it say Fort Comfy on it?"

"Because it's a cabin-fort," Abby said. "Maggie has one too, and we'll be at Camp Pillow Fort for the rest of the summer."

"The rest of the summer, huh?" said Alex. He leaned on the doorframe, his arms crossed over his Impressionist Water Lilies apron. "And we only just got you back today. I hope we'll still get to see you two while you're attending Camp Pillow Fort."

"You will," I said. "We'll stop by to say hi sometimes."

"Glad to hear it. But for now, dinner will be ready in five—nope, now it's four minutes. Are you finished unpacking, Abby?"

Abby yanked a final bundle out of the suitcase on her bed and flipped the lid shut.

"Yes!" she said, raising both hands above her head. "Victory! Done before dinner."

"Then I'll see you girls, and your freshly washed hands, at the table in three and a half minutes," said Alex, and he left.

"That's just enough time for you to open this," Abby said, tossing the final bundle at me. I unrolled it. It was a mustard-yellow Camp Cantaloupe T-shirt, with the name of the camp in red letters over half a cantaloupe and the outline of Orcas Island.

"Hey, thanks," I said, running a hand over the logo and trying to figure out if I felt happy or sad. "Now I can look like someone who went to summer camp." I turned the shirt around. On the back was a picture of the same goofy-looking moose from Abby's postcard, with the words *Cantaloupe Cantaloupe, Moose Moose Moose* in a half circle around it.

"What's this all about?" I asked, holding it up. After all those boring stories, this looked like it might actually be interesting. This had secret code written all over it.

"Seriously?" said Abby. "Did I not tell you about the

moose? I am such a terrible friend. That's, like, the heart and soul of Camp Cantaloupe. Okay, so apparently years and years ago—"

But the story had to wait, as Alex called out a two-minute warning and we were off, racing Abby's brothers down the hall to dinner.

* * *

We ate out on the patio next to the twins' broken bike "art installation." We had grilled pork, corn salsa, red cabbage coleslaw, and sandwiches made of Rice Krispies treats and peach ice cream for dessert. Abby couldn't stop talking about how good the food was after six weeks of the mess hall, and her dad and brothers pestered her for all the best camp stories, so lucky me, I got to hear them a second time.

Moths came out and fluttered around the table, and the sky had faded from pink to gold to indigo before dinner wound down.

"Can Maggie stay the night, Dad?" asked Abby, scraping up the last bit of salsa with Rice Krispies treat crumbs.

"Sure, if your mom says it's okay, Maggie," said Alex.

"She won't be home until late," I said. "But I can run over and leave her a note."

I helped Abby and her brothers clear the table, then went back through the gap in the fence to my dark, empty house. It felt extra dark and empty after Abby's. I grabbed my toothbrush and pajamas and scribbled a note at the kitchen counter.

> Mom, Abby's home. I'm asking permission to spend the night at her place. Yes, her dad is there. Yes, I said thank you. Yes, I'm bringing my toothbrush. I'll probably be hanging out with Abby all day tomorrow, too. Have a good night/day at work.

Outside I could hear the birds finishing their nighttime songs, but inside the only sound was my footsteps as I turned off the lights one by one on my way to the door.

"Good night, fort formerly known as Gromit's Room," I called as I passed the living room and Fort McForterson. "I'm sleeping at Abby's tonight, but I still love you and I'll be back tomorrow."

I turned off the last light and put a hand on the front doorknob.

There was a soft rustle behind me.

I stopped.

Everything was still.

"Hello?" I said into the darkness.

Silence. One cold finger danced down the back of my neck.

I must have been imagining things. Probably just my

shoes squeaking on the floor. No way was it a knife-wielding zombie counterspy, or a giant northwestern shadow leech. No way. I turned and reached for the door again.

A soft, distinct thump sounded from the living room.

I spun around as cold fear leaped out of the dark and wrapped around me like a blanket. All my senses snapped into high gear.

I wasn't alone.

What should I do? For real? I wasn't making up adventures here. There was *someone in the house with me.* And it sounded like they were in my fort. I stood frozen by the door, staring into the darkness, my eyes so wide they hurt.

Okay, what would my mom do? She was always good in a crisis. What had she said on the phone earlier? *Deep, slow breath, you'll be fine.*

I forced myself to take a breath and let it out silently. I took another, and a warming spark of irritation appeared along with it.

Why should I be the one scared? This was *my* house, wasn't it? And even if someone—or some*thing*, said an unhelpful voice in the back my head—was lurking inside my pillow fort, I was eleven and a half years old, and I had a lifetime of experience dealing with crisis and danger.

Okay fine, maybe that had been mostly imaginary, but I still had plenty of practice. This wasn't all that different from the time last winter when Abby was being held captive in a ski lodge in the Alps and I had to take on a room full of elite werewolf guards single-handed. A big show of confidence saved the day there; maybe it would work again.

I darted across the room in four quick steps and flicked on the overhead light.

"Who's there? You're surrounded. Show yourself!"

Nothing. No movement, no sound from the fort.

"Fine," I said, ignoring my painfully thudding heart. Deep, slow breath. "Then we're coming in."

Trying to sound like as many people as possible, I clomp-stomped across the floor to the fort. The sign declaring *Fort McForterson* was hanging crooked. It looked strange now, almost like a warning. I'd never realized before just how much my fort looked like a nest, a nest for some squirming, overgrown rat-people with poisonous claws and curved teeth and horrible hairy. . . .

Whoa, Maggie, rally. Another deep breath. It was still *my* overgrown rat-people nest, and no one had a right to be in there but me.

I crouched down, ready to jump back if anything spiny came flying out, and instantly wished I had something more impressive than a sparkly blue toothbrush and a pair of sleepy dinosaur pajama pants to defend myself with.

But hey, maybe I just heard a book falling over. This really could be nothing at all, right?

A slow ripple ran across the fort's bedsheet ceiling, inches from my face.

Oh. No.

It couldn't.

THREE

There was definitely something. Absolutely definitely an unknown something, inside my pillow fort.

I lifted a shaking hand toward the entrance flap with my breath caught in my throat. But before I could get there, something parted the flap from the *inside* . . .

. . . and Samson sauntered out.

My mouth dropped open and my butt hit the floor.

Samson banged against my knee, purring. He had a piece of craft paper stuck to his snagglepaw.

"Samson, buddy," I said, weak with relief. "What are you doing here?"

He head-butted me again. I tugged the paper from his paw, racking my brain for an explanation. Had he followed me over and snuck in behind me? Maybe . . . only no, I would have heard him clattering on the wood floor.

But how else could he be there?

I crawled into the fort to look for clues, the patchwork scarf brushing over my shoulder, and . . . and . . .

Hey, what was going on here?

The pillow Abby had knocked over earlier was lying on its side again, only instead of chair legs behind it there was another pillow. An orange-plaid pillow. With light seeping around its edges. Light coming from . . . someplace else.

As I sat there, gaping, Samson ambled past me into the fort, headed straight for the crack of light, slipped through it, and vanished.

"Okaaay," I said to the world at large. "Oh-kay."

Once more with the deep, slow breaths. Then I followed the cat.

I crawled into the fort, gave the new pillow a push . . .

. . . and found myself looking directly into Fort Comfy.

Ever since we were little, Abby and I had played long, intricate adventure games. In the last one before camp stole her away, we were explorers hunting for giant sapphires in the Lost Temple of the Saber-Toothed Tiger. Everything was going well until we reached the treasury, where we just couldn't decode the strange stripey markings covering the walls. It wasn't until I whapped one with a stick and smelled oranges that we realized the entire temple was scratch and sniff. After that, finding the secret chamber of sapphires was easy. Although getting out again wasn't when Abby accidentally released the Saber-Toothed Guardians from the sleep ray I'd trapped them in when we arrived. Luckily, I had a spare hang glider in my bag, because even in our custom-designed adventures something could always go wrong. And I was nothing if not a seasoned veteran.

But this right here? Right now? To have it happening in real life? To actually be able to reach from my fort straight into Abby's next door and scratch Samson's chin? Not even my years of advanced tactical training could prepare me for that. I stared at the space betwen our forts, feeling almost seasick as my brain heaved back and forth between *This can't be happening!* and *Open your eyes, it is!*

I crawled forward, steeling myself for a tingle or shock or shiver of energy, but there was only the soft rumble of Samson's purring and Creepy Frog googly-eyeing me from under the squashy blanket pile.

Completely dazed, I kept moving and clambered to my feet in Abby's bedroom. She wasn't there.

I stepped into the hall. The bathroom door opened.

"Hey, Mags," said Abby. She'd redone her new side braid. "What took you so long?"

I opened my mouth, then shut it again.

"Did you want to brush your teeth?" Abby asked.

I looked down, realizing I still had my toothbrush and pajamas tucked under one arm. How on earth was I going to explain what had just happened?

Answer: I wasn't.

I grabbed Abby's arm and pulled her into her room.

"Okay," I said as she opened her mouth to protest. "Do you remember when we were parachuting into Oldfang Cathedral to find the lost relic of St. Claudia that held the secret code for the bank vault in Switzerland?"

Abby gave a half smile. "It's kind of late to start a game now, isn't it, Mags?"

"Do you remember?" I insisted. She frowned a little, fingering her braid, thinking. My heart gave a twinge. Old Abby wouldn't have had to think. "Come on," I said. "There were thirty of SCAR's best secret agents trying to get there before us. . . ."

"And only you knew about the hidden door in the kitchen staircase. Okay, yeah, I remember. Why?"

"Because what I'm about to show you is like that parachute jump," I said. "I need you to trust me here."

The corners of Abby's mouth twitched. "Okay," she said. "Sure."

She crouched down beside me, and I waved her into the fort, following right behind. The little lamp lit up the mounds of blankets, purring Samson, Creepy Frog, and, directly across from us . . .

"Hey!" said Abby, stopping dead. "What?!"

Her mouth dropped open. She looked over at me.

"I know," I said.

"But—I mean, what?" She crawled through the gap into Fort McForterson, poked her head out of the entrance flap, and crawled back, her eyes shining.

"Mags, this is . . . We're . . . we're *linked!*"

"Uh-huh. And you know what we've got to do now, right?"

"Obviously." Abby nodded. "Test the cucumber casserole out of it."

So we did, going back and forth between the forts over and over and over. And no matter what we tried—whether the pillows were shut on one side or the other, if we were both in Abby's fort or mine, if the fort lamps were on or off—one fort always led to the other. We even checked to see if having Samson around made any difference, but it didn't seem to.

"Okay, I can't believe I'm actually about to say this," said Abby as we finally settled down in Fort McForterson, "but this is magic, isn't it?"

"Oof." I shook my head. "We don't know that for sure. And calling it *magic* makes us sound like third graders. Let's just call it *linking*, like you did before."

"Got it," said Abby. "So, how do we think this *linking* happened?"

"Well, let's start with what we know," I said. "We know I had a fort the whole time you were gone and it never linked anywhere. Now you come home, we build your fort, and suddenly they're connected." I looked at her seriously. "Maybe it's you."

"Me?" Abby's eyes went wide. "We learned a ton of stuff at Camp Cantaloupe, Mags, but we didn't learn that."

A loud knocking floated through the link from Abby's room. "Hello? Girls?"

"Oop!" Abby sat bolt upright. "We've got company. Back to Fort Comfy!" She dove through the link. I scrambled after her.

"Hey, Dad. What's up?" Abby said, poking her head out of the fort.

"Hey," said Alex, as I smooshed in beside her. "Oh, hi, Maggie. I must've missed you coming back over. Were you two telling ghost stories or something in there?"

"Yes," Abby said. "Ghost stories. Absolutely."

"Ghost stories," I said. "Yes."

"Absolutely."

"Sounds good," said Alex. "But I hope they weren't too scary; it's just about time for lights-out."

"I still need to brush my teeth," I said.

"All right, but five minutes to bedtime, okay?"

Alex left, and we changed into our pajamas.

Abby was already in bed as I came back from the bathroom. I switched off the overhead light and settled into the fort. Abby rolled up on one elbow. "Dude, I seriously cannot wait for tomorrow," she said. "Can you even imagine how much fun our camp is gonna be now? I was worried the rest of summer might be boring after Camp Cantaloupe, but this changes evvvv-ry-thing."

I froze, halfway snuggled in. I couldn't believe my ears. Did Abby really just say she'd thought the precious, glorious half of summer she got to spend reunited with me was going to be boring?

"Seriously," Abby said, rolling over. "Camp Pillow Fort for the win."

I clicked off the lamp and lay back, staring up at the ceiling. Old Abby didn't know the meaning of the word *boring*, but it looked like New Abby did. She'd really changed a ton at camp, or maybe camp had changed her.

At least we were together now, though. That was the most important thing. And we had weeks and weeks to have adventures in. Just the two of us, like always. Like it should be. New Abby would come around.

I stretched my feet through the link and wiggled my toes back and forth. *My house, Abby's house. My house, Abby's house.* It was just like that time my mom and I drove to Idaho, and I spent a full ten minutes hopping back and forth over the state line. Only this border here included the obvious potential for midnight kitchen raids, neverending sleepovers, and glorious prank wars on cute teenage older brothers.

I rolled over and grinned into the dark. We were going to get into so much trouble.

FOUR

Alex was leaning against the counter eating cereal as Abby and I stumbled into the kitchen the next morning.

"Hey, it's my favorite girls!" he said. "You two are up early. Big exciting plans today?"

Abby caught my eye. I tried to hide my smile in a yawn.

"Not really," Abby said, pulling bowls out of the cupboard. "We're just going to hang out at Maggie's and work on our cabins."

"Oh, that's right. You're heading back to camp," said Alex. "Well, I'll miss you. Don't forget you promised you'd stop by from time to time."

Abby nodded. "We'll be around. Today's just for setup, anyway."

"Just reinforcing the links," I said, getting out spoons.

"That's very poetic, Maggie," said Alex. Abby snorted into the fridge.

"Do *you* have big exciting plans today?" I asked Alex.

"Oh, I thought I'd work on the lawn, and then I've got some errands. And, uh." He looked down. "Tamal's coming over for dinner tonight."

"Yeah?" Abby said, her head popping up. "Are you two dating now or something?"

Alex's cheeks arced into a grin, and he knocked over the cereal box. "Um, yes," he said, hastily fumbling it back upright.

"Finally," said Abby, handing me the orange juice. "I like him."

Alex smiled adorably down into his bowl. "So do I," he said.

Breakfast didn't take long, and soon Abby and I were settling into the arts-and-crafts corner of Fort McForterson to hammer out the details of our new game.

"I can't believe how many postcards you have," Abby said, running a finger over the shoe box. "Did I really send you all these?"

"Mostly," I said. "The ones in back are from my uncle Joe. He's been up in Alaska since April, doing this whale research project."

"Ooh, cool," said Abby. "Can I read one?"

I shrugged. Abby pulled out a card with a picture of a snowy mountain range on the front.

April 29th

Dear Maggie, there was a meteor shower last night. The whole top of the sky filled with shining trails of silver. It was unbelievable. If I ever get tired of whales, I'm going to become an astronomer. There's already a whale constellation, so I could start there, although I would miss writing hundred-page papers about whale poop. I hope you get a chance to come see this place someday. You would totally love it.

Love, Uncle Joe

"Aww, he misses you," said Abby, shoving the card back into the box. "Do you think you'll go visit him?"

I handed her a pen and a pad of paper. "Nah, my mom would never let me go. He's in this remote cabin way up on the edge of the Arctic Circle. He had to take a plane, a ferry, a train, a bus, *and* a pickup truck just to get out there."

"Whoa," said Abby. "All he's missing is a ride on a moose." She looked up. "Hey! I still have to tell you the story of the Camp Cantaloupe moose! It's the very best story ever! Here, let me get comfortable."

Um, okay. Hey there, New Abby.

Abby rolled over onto her stomach and pushed her feet through the link. "This place is so much better now that we've got two rooms," she said. "Love it. Okay, so, this is the story the camp director told us:

"Camp Cantaloupe was founded a long, long time ago, over half a century, and originally it wasn't called Camp Cantaloupe, it was called Camp Orcas after the island. One night in the middle of its first summer this massive storm came through, and the next morning the beaches were covered with all this wreckage and debris that washed up on shore, along with a super confused moose that people figured must have gotten blown down from Canada. Big huge storm. Big huge mess.

"The campers back then volunteered to help clean up the beaches if they could keep all the cool stuff they found, so they did and they used it to build the most incredible tree house. The moose kept wandering around the beaches watching them while they worked, and I guess it got used to having company, because when they were done, it followed them back to camp and stayed there.

"Everyone loved the moose and tried to feed it from their lunches, but the only thing it would ever take was . . . ta-da, cantaloupe! So they gave the moose all the cantaloupe they had, and it became the camp pet. And it must have loved them

as much as they loved it, because when the kids and counselors went home in the fall, the people who lived on the island said the moose got really sad and wouldn't eat anything. And that winter it died of a broken heart."

I couldn't help it—I laughed. Abby shushed me.

"The next summer all the returning kids showed up with cantaloupes, because of course they were excited to see the moose again, and when they heard the news, they couldn't believe their favorite moose in the whole world was gone. People were so sad, they talked about canceling camp. But soon stories started going around about kids seeing the moose at night, peering through the windows of the cabins, all eyes and antlers and big huge nostrils. Kids even left their cantaloupes outside for it, and the next morning they were always gone.

"Then one day a girl got lost in the woods and everyone was worried, but that night she turned up at camp safe and sound and told everyone the moose found her and showed her the way back, leading her through the trees. From then on everyone hoped they would see the friendly ghost moose, and they voted to change the name and motto and everything, and that's why the official camp call is . . . Cantaloupe Cantaloupe, Moose Moose Moose!"

I blinked at her. Seriously, a fruit-loving ghost moose that blew in on a dark and stormy night? That was the *best story ever*? The big, mysterious legend of Camp Cantaloupe? I'd come up with better stories while brushing my teeth.

"Neat," I said. "That's really . . . neat. So, did you ever see it?"

"Not the moose, no," Abby said. "But I hung out in the tree house all the time. That's where the camp director told us first-timers the story. You would seriously love this tree house, Mags. It's all made out of driftwood and planks and window frames and things. It even has this trapdoor with a real old-timey lock, although it's stuck shut, so you have to go around and over the side to get in the tree house. But once you're there you can see over Puget Sound to the other islands, and on clear days you can see Canada. It was my favorite place in the entire camp, and that's saying a lot."

Abby reached back with her foot and flipped Creepy Frog over her head. "The director went to Camp Cantaloupe when he was our age," she continued. "He said it's camp tradition to sit in the tree house on your very first day, eat cantaloupe, and hear the story of the moose. Hey!" Her eyes lit up. "We should have one too!"

"What, a weird fruit tradition?" I said

Abby whapped me with Creepy Frog. "No, a camp director. I nominate you."

"Wait, me?"

"Sure," said Abby. "I mean, you built the first fort. And you like running things more than me."

I looked down at my hands, trying to keep my smile under control. This was perfect! I was great at running things, and as director I could start steering us away from summer camp games ASAP. But I didn't want to make New Abby suspicious. How to accept power without sounding too eager?

A bass rumbling filled the fort, and I looked up. Samson had arrived from Fort Comfy, strolling up and over Abby's back with a square of toilet paper stuck to his paw.

"Ow! Honestly, Samson." Abby twisted and grabbed him. "What now, toilet paper? Where did you get that? You're like the garbage-collector-in-chief."

"Ooh! Perfect!" I said, spotting my chance. "Why don't we make Samson our director instead?"

"Samson?"

"Yeah. He's around all the time, and he's definitely a fan of the forts."

"Ha! Cute idea," said Abby. "All in favor?" We raised our hands. "Motion passed. Congratulations, Samson." She shook Samson's tail.

"I guess we still need someone to manage meetings and stuff, though," I said casually. "Maybe a vice director, or something . . ."

"Well, that's you, then," said Abby.

"You're sure?" *Don't smile, Maggie.*

"Obviously. All in favor of Maggie being vice director of Camp Pillow Fort?" She stuck a hand in the air and raised Samson's tail with the other. "Awesome. Motion also passed. Where do you— Hey, no, Mr. Director! Leave it!" Samson was batting happily at the patchwork scarf hanging above the entrance. Abby seized him, barricading him in her arms, and he settled down, purring like a lawn mower.

"All right," I said, brandishing my pen. Excellent. It was my turn now. "If that's all the moose-storytelling and leader-electing business out of the way, let's get started on this game—camp—thing."

"Hooray," said Abby. "What should we do first?"

I gave her a look. "Are you serious?" Don't do this to me, New Abby. "You know the answer to that."

Abby smiled and rubbed Samson's head with her chin. "'All good games start with a map,'" she said, quoting my long-standing policy. I gave a sigh of relief.

We divided up the work. Abby did the actual drawing, since she had the art and graphic-design superpowers, while I surveyed the forts and picked out colored pencils.

Abby did a beautiful job. She put our forts side by side right in the center of the map, making sure to draw in the correct number of pillows, and outlined the whole thing in a border of sheets and blankets. In the blank spaces at the edges she wrote *Here There Be Margins*, which she said was an inside joke from camp. I decided not to ask what that was about.

All good maps are supposed to be jagged at the edges, technically speaking, but the crimping scissors I stole from my mom were missing, so we had to settle for artistically ripping the paper instead. Abby added a picture of Creepy Frog in one corner for scale, and another of Samson with his tail pointing north for a compass, and our map was complete.

"Dude," said Abby, running a finger over Fort Comfy. "Look at how many unlinked pillows we have. Hey, what if they all went somewhere? There could be another fort here, and here, and here. We could go so many cool places!"

"Cool places?" She had me just a pillow fort away. Wasn't that enough? "What sort of cool places?"

"Anywhere! Come on—use your famous imagination, Mags." She counted off on her fingers. "We could have links to the pool, the museum, the library, the teachers' lounge at school next year, both ice cream shops, the Roller Derby rink, that one amazing costume shop, the aquarium . . ."

I gaped at her. That was brilliant. Although my highly trained brain already saw a problem. "Okay," I said, "but wouldn't we have to somehow get to all those places and build pillow forts in them first?"

"What do you mean?"

"Well, our forts only connect to each other, not to other rooms in our houses, right? So there probably always needs to be a fort on the other end to connect to. And I seriously doubt there's already a pillow fort hidden in the aquarium waiting for us."

"Shoot," said Abby, "fair point. Well, I hope we figure it out and find a way to add more forts and people soon."

"What, Samson and I aren't good enough for you anymore?" I asked, only half joking.

Abby suddenly became very interested in smoothing out a corner of the map. "Of course you are. It's just that, you know, two people and a cat isn't much of a camp, is it? If we had more campers, we could really do it right. And that would mean we'd have more cabins, too." She tapped the paper. "I mean, how cool would it be if somebody else *did* have a fort somewhere, like some kid nearby. What if we were linked in already and we just didn't know it yet?" She looked around hopefully at the pillows lining the walls.

"That would be awesome," I said. Except obviously it wouldn't. I'd only just gotten Abby back; I wasn't about to start sharing her with someone new. "But it's pretty much impossible."

"Yeah, I guess." Abby sighed. She cuddled Samson closer. "They'd probably need some sort of connection with us, not just a fort of their own. And I've been gone all summer, so that's no good. And you haven't really been in touch with anybody at all, right?"

I nodded. She didn't have to say it like that, but it was true. "Only my mom," I said. "And, ugh, tennis lessons—I never did learn those kids' names—and Caitlin for like a second, and you, but no one else except . . . hey . . . maybe . . ."

FIVE

Abby beat me to the punch. "Your uncle!" she cried, pointing dramatically at the postcard box. "Your uncle Jim, Mags!"

"Uncle Joe."

"Your uncle Joe, Mags! He's been sending you postcards, right? And you've been writing back from inside your fort?"

"Well, yeah," I said. "Only I really don't think—"

But Samson was upended with a yowl as Abby jumped up and started pulling pillows aside.

"Hey, hang on," I said. What if she brought the whole place down? What if she collapsed the link? What if the collapsing link sucked us down with it into some blankety underworld? "Uncle Joe probably doesn't even have a—"

"BINGO!" cried Abby, clenching a wall pillow in one hand, pointing dramatically with the other at a completely out-of-place gray cushion filling the gap.

I goggled.

"But—but this doesn't make sense," I said. "Why would Uncle Joe have a pillow fort?"

"Why not?" said Abby, a massive smile on her face. "Maybe you gave him the idea in one of your postcards and he thought it sounded fun, and whatever's making them all connect is affecting his, now." She held out a hand to the strange gray cushion. "So, after you!"

I shook my head. This was happening way too fast.

"Hold on, hold on," I said. "Just wait a second. There's no proof that link goes to Uncle Joe's fort. None. What if it goes to a . . . a haunted platinum mine instead? Or a space station that had a massive hull breach and there's no more oxygen? Or an underwater trench full of razor-backed assassin crabs? What if I go through that pillow and never come back?"

Abby raised her eyebrows. "Seriously? Earth to Maggie. This isn't one of your games. This is real life, and it must be your uncle through there because who else could it be? And since he's your relative, I thought it would be polite if you went first. But if you're scared . . ." She turned to the gray cushion.

"No, no, it's okay," I said. "I get it. I'm vice director. I should go first." Abby lowered her eyebrows and sat back.

I took a deep, slow breath, preparing for the worst, and crawled forward into the mysterious fort.

And immediately almost threw up, because *I was facing the wrong way.*

From my perspective, I'd just pushed forward into a gray cushion standing on its side. But it turned out that from the perspective of the new fort, I was actually *under* the cushion, meaning my entire world gave a quarter turn *up* and *back* in the space of about two seconds. It was not my favorite sensation.

"How-nuh-whaha?!" I said, clutching at the pillow.

"What is it?" asked Abby behind—or, no, beneath me. "Is it a spaceship full of oxygen crabs? Are you dead?"

I ignored her and tried to get my bearings.

I wasn't in a spaceship, or in an underwater trench, but I wasn't in a pillow fort, either. I was on a sofa, under a musty-smelling blanket that seemed to be just lying there normal style. Light was seeping through around the edges, but no sounds were coming from the room or spaceport or whatever was outside to give me any clues. It was just me and the sofa and the blanket and silence.

It was strange. Very strange. Without a pillow fort how had I linked to wherever I was? I left my legs dangling back in Seattle in case I needed to make a speedy getaway and felt around carefully in the gloom. My hand hit something: a small, stiff piece of paper.

"I think I found a clue," I called back—or down, heaving

myself all the way up through the link. I sat beside the gap, squinting at the paper in the dim light, and my stomach gave a happy lurch as I recognized the last postcard I'd sent Uncle Joe.

"Hey, you were right!" I called. I tucked the card back between the pillows, slipped out from under the blanket, and emerged into what was absolutely without a shadow of a doubt my uncle's cabin.

Okay, this was awesome.

The cabin was small, just two rooms. The one I was in held the sofa, a desk covered with notebooks and electronic equipment, and a twin bed. The other had a basic kitchen setup with mini appliances, two folding chairs, and a tiny table. The place smelled old and musty and might have been completely boring, except for the whales plastered over absolutely everything.

Poster-size glossy photos covered the walls: whales diving, whales swimming, whales leaping, whales slapping the water with their fins. There were smaller photos tacked up between them, filling every corner, and even more piled on the table and spilling onto the floor. Most of them had official-looking numbers across the bottom, so they were probably important scientific documents, but Uncle Joe had them pinned up on every surface like a teenager obsessing over a favorite band.

I felt a rush of affection for my dorky uncle. If I had to share Abby and our linked-up forts with someone, he was the only acceptable choice.

"Well, I almost puked," said Abby, clambering out of the sofa. "We could totally charge kids good money for that ride! How weird that your fort just linked to a regular sofa, though."

I looked back at the sofa. It definitely was weird. How on earth did a cushion with a blanket over it count as a fort? And what was making it all work? We had to figure it out soon. We'd been lucky to end up somewhere safe, but if the rules were this loose, well, things could go wrong—very, very quickly.

Abby whapped me on the arm. "Dude, stop staring at that sofa like it's possessed," she said. "We can figure it out later. C'mon, we're in Alaska!"

She ran around exploring every corner of the cabin, discovering a closet full of cold-weather gear and a door to a tiny bathroom papered with more photos. "I guess your uncle's not that into whales, huh?" she said. "I wonder where he is, anyway."

"Out researching, I guess."

We went to the window over the desk.

"Whoa, that view," said Abby. "I would love to work up here."

It was a bright, clear day. The window in the main room showed rocky arctic tundra turning into craggy hills, then snow-covered mountains in the distance. We ran to look out the window over the kitchen sink and saw more of the same, plus a rusty red pickup truck and a shed that looked like it might hold a generator. But it was the window in the front of the cabin that had the real view: a beach of black rock and silver-blue ice curling around a dark, gleaming, wave-flecked bay.

"It's just like the pictures on his postcards," I said, drinking in the light and the water and the great big sky. My heart began pumping hard. For the first time all summer I was free. No more filling in time, no more bumming around my house and yard waiting for Abby to get back and my summer to start. I was stepping out into the wide world. I could already see myself striding across this beach, my head held high, seagulls flocking to my call, and the sun shining down as I went to meet my destiny with the wind blowing through my hair.

"Look, there he is!" said Abby, pointing to a motorboat bobbing out in the bay.

She pulled open the front door, and we ran down the steps, shouted in shock, and ran right back in.

"Man! It's freezing in Alaska!" Abby said. We raided the closet, bundling up in coats and hats and sweaters at least three sizes too big, and headed outdoors again. The air was fresh beyond belief and smelled like seaweed and stone and cold salt water.

We clattered down the rocks to the shore and jumped up and down, waving our arms and yelling. The figure in the boat didn't look up.

"I think he's wearing headphones or something," I said, holding a hand over my eyes. "And he's not looking this way. How are we supposed to let him know we're here?"

"On it!" said Abby. She grabbed a baseball-size chunk of ice in each hand and flung them as far out into the bay as she could, which, seeing as it was Abby, was pretty far. There were two big splashes. The figure in the boat lifted its head. If I hadn't already known it was Uncle Joe, the yell that echoed across the water would have told me for sure.

"Holy whale poop!"

Uncle Joe tugged the motor to life and turned his boat toward shore. We waited, hopping around to keep warm.

"Hang on—wait a second," Abby said suddenly. "What exactly are we doing here?"

"What do you mean?"

"I mean what are we going to say when he gets here? Are we telling him everything? Are we letting him in on our discovery?"

"Ooh, right!" I said.

"I'm not sure we should. What if he goes all grown-up on us and tries to take control of the forts?"

I shook my head. "He wouldn't do that. He's not that kind of guy."

"Good. I guess we should probably just tell him, then? He'll want to know how we got up here, and it's not like we have a cover story."

We turned back to the water just as Uncle Joe pulled the boat up onto the rocks. I expected him to be surprised, maybe even shocked, but as we ran to meet him, he shouted something I never thought I would hear come out of his mouth.

"Not one word, either of you! Not one single beluga-bawling word about it!"

"Hi— You—huh?" I said. "Not one word about what?"

"Anything!" said Uncle Joe, putting his hands on his hips. "I don't want to know a whale-burping thing about anything at all!"

Abby looked at me in alarm.

"But . . . ," I said, "aren't you wondering how we got up—"

"LALALA!" cried Uncle Joe, shoving his fingers in his ears.

It took both of us putting our hands over our mouths to get him to stop la-la-ing and explain himself.

"Okay," he said, eyeing us carefully. "Maggie. And Abby, I'm guessing?" Abby nodded. "Good. That's good. Nice to meet you. I'm Joe. Now, are you two clear on why I don't want you to say anything just yet?"

We shook our heads.

Uncle Joe ran a hand over his face. "All right. Maggie, you know from my postcards that I've been up here all on my own for three months. And apart from a few day trips into town for supplies, I've spent most of that time sitting by myself, in a boat, watching the clouds and listening to the underwater microphones. Take a moment to imagine that for me." He spread his arms wide, and Abby and I looked around at the sky and rocks and waves.

"And now imagine that two young people, who you know should definitely be back in Seattle, have suddenly appeared in front of you here beside your remote Alaskan bay. What would you think?"

We looked at each other.

"You'd think you were hallucinating, that's what," Uncle Joe answered for us. "You'd think you were hallucinating and actually having a conversation with a flock of seagulls or a pile of rocks or something, and that's just not a good use of time. So you would hope, against all your scientific training, that you weren't hallucinating and these young people actually were there, which would mean some kind of magic was involved—"

"Actually, we're not calling it magic," I cut in, "because—"

"WHICH MEANS," said Uncle Joe, shouting over me, "that I don't want to hear a single word about it!"

Our shock must have shown on our faces, because he spoke more gently as he went on.

"Listen, kids. Maggie, Abby. I may be a grown-up now, but I've read a ton of books in my time, and I know how these things go. The moment the kids in stories tell the grown-ups about the magic they've discovered is always the moment things start to go seriously wrong. I'm guessing you've probably done some very hard work and been brave and smart and you want to tell me all about it, but the only way I'm willing to let you stay here is if you agree to act like you being here is completely and totally normal. Can you do that for me?"

There was a huge, windy silence. I had no idea what to say, but Abby tugged her fancy new braid out from under her hat, put her hands on her hips, and smiled.

"So, Joe," she said. "What are we having for lunch?"

SIX

After a lunch of canned soup and crackers, which was pretty much all Uncle Joe had for food, came "Everything You Ever Wanted to Know about Whales," an Uncle Joe afternoon lecture. I listened from the folding table while Abby followed Uncle Joe around the cabin, hanging on to his every word as he gushed about the pictures covering the walls.

"Ooh, and this one here," said Uncle Joe, tapping a photo next to the fridge, "is Bertha. She's a fighter. See that massive lateral scar on her tail? She probably got that in a fight with an orca when she was young. And this photo shows a bubble net, a sort of ring of bubbles humpbacks make underwater to confuse fish and trap them in a small space so they can eat them. Whales also slap the surface of the water to send down sound waves to freak the fish out. You really should see a whale calf try to slap the water sometime—it's the cutest thing in the whole world."

I smiled. I felt good. I was on an adventure, I was warm and full, and it looked like the combination of cold Alaskan air and my dorky-sweet uncle had finally driven Camp Cantaloupe clear out of Abby's mind. At this rate, I'd be able to steer us back to our regularly scheduled programming in no time.

Abby came over to the table and sat down across from me. "I just realized something funny," she whispered. Uncle Joe was still chatting away.

"What?"

"You and your uncle have been, like, your own tiny club of zany people living by themselves in cabins all summer. Isn't that hilarious?"

Ugh. So much for hanging on Uncle Joe's every word.

"First off," I whispered back, "you are exactly as zany as me, Miss I-made-my-best-friend-a-scarf-in-the-middle-of-July."

"Hey, you made one too!"

"Second, my fort wasn't a *cabin*"—I pulled out my extra-strength air quotes—"until you came home and decided to turn it into one."

"Okay, fair. But you totally agreed to it."

"And third, where have you been living all summer? Oh, that's right: a cabin!"

"Well, yeah," Abby said. "That's my point. You're supposed to live in a cabin at camp. It's kinda weird when you're on your own."

"And this big guy," said Uncle Joe, waving at a column of glossy pictures beside the front door, "is our grand finale. His name is Orpheus. He's the whole reason I'm out here."

Abby looked up, her braid swinging. "Orpheus? That guy from the old Greek legends?" I stared at her. She shrugged. "One of the counselors at camp read us some of the stories."

"That's wonderful," Uncle Joe said. "Do you know the story, Maggie?"

"Nope." Whee, I was all on my own again.

"Orpheus was a singer," explained Uncle Joe. "An amazing singer. The best. He was so good, he almost managed to sing the love of his life back from the dead. And I think Orpheus the whale is doing something just as incredible."

"You think he's singing dead whales back to life?" asked Abby.

"Ha! No, nothing like that, but I think he's what I call a rogue singer."

"And what's a rogue singer?" I asked, figuring I might as well keep being the one who didn't know anything.

Uncle Joe plonked down on the back of the sofa. "Well, with humpbacks it's the adult males who do the singing, and they usually sing more or less the same song that changes slowly over time. We've got lots of recordings of different whales singing over the years, and we think we basically understand what most songs are all about. But based on some clues I've come across in my research, I think that during summer feeding time, which is right now, one or two very rare whales leave the group to sing a one-hundred-percent *different* song all by themselves. Orpheus definitely keeps wandering off on his own, and I want to be the first scientist to get a recording of this other song. If there is one.

"I'm basically the only whale researcher on the planet who believes any of this, though. All my colleagues think I'm totally weird, but I can live with that."

"You, um, might not have much choice," I said, gesturing around at the walls.

Uncle Joe threw a pillow at me.

"Stop!" Abby and I shouted, leaping to our feet.

Uncle Joe was sitting right beside the blanket and pillow that made up the link. If he moved one more pillow or even leaned the wrong way, he would see the gap. Or worse, fall straight through, destroying the link and leaving us stranded up here for good.

Uncle Joe froze like a fish in a bubble net.

"What do we do?" I hissed at Abby, forgetting I was annoyed. This was a crisis.

"We've got to build something more secure," Abby whispered back. I nodded.

"So, um, hey, Uncle Joe," I said in my best casual voice. "I'm not saying anything in particular here, but this might be a good time for you to go be, you know, somewhere else for a while."

Uncle Joe's eyebrows went up, then down, then back up again. "Okay..."

"How about you go for a walk on the beach?" suggested Abby. "You can look for wildlife or something. Maybe you'll see a moose!" She nudged my leg under the table.

Ugh, she was thinking of that ghost moose again. What, did she expect to see it prancing around Uncle Joe's cabin up here on the edge of the Arctic Circle? We were already having a bigger adventure than anything Camp Cantaloupe could possibly offer. Why couldn't she just let it go already?

"All right, I'll do that," said Uncle Joe. "But sorry, Abby, there aren't any moose up here this time of year. How, uh, how long should my wildlife walk be...?"

"Fifteen minutes should do it," I said.

"I'll just change my sweater."

The moment Uncle Joe trooped out into the cold Alaska afternoon, Abby and I leaped into action, tearing apart the sofa to build a proper fort around the link, with a door and blanket roof and everything. It wasn't the most beautiful pillow fort the world had ever seen, but it would have to do.

Uncle Joe gave the fort a long look when he came back in.

"I'm doing my best not to think about what any of this means, kids," he said with a sigh, rubbing the back of his neck, "but it's not easy. I'm guessing there are all sorts of rules I'm not supposed to break or things I'm not supposed to do, right? No, don't answer that—you'll probably say too much." He chewed his lip. "Okay, here's the deal: I won't mess with this fort so long as you two promise to announce your presence whenever you, uh, swing by."

"Like, knock on the floor or something?" I said.

"That'll work," said Uncle Joe. "But make sure to knock loudly, just in case I'm in the bath."

Abby raised her hand. "Is it saying too much if I mention you should think up a name for your fort?"

Uncle Joe flinched. "Well, it's too late now if it is." He eyed the heap of pillows and blankets, then smiled. "At least that's easy." He went over to the desk, scribbled something on a piece of paper, and held it up.

"Fort Orpheus," read Abby. "I like it."

"It's perfect," I said.

Uncle Joe beamed.

The three of us hung out for the rest of the afternoon, talking about sciency science and whales and Alaska and watching the sun shine down on the waves. Uncle Joe was telling me about the scientists who had stayed in the cabin before him and all the random gear they'd left behind, when

Abby, who had run home to feed Samson, came bursting back out of the fort.

"Hey, Joe, cover your ears for a minute, will you?" she said.

Uncle Joe squeezed his eyes shut, put his fingers in his ears, and started humming.

"What's up?" I asked.

"We've gotta go," said Abby. "My dad says dinner's almost ready."

"Do we have to?" I wasn't ready to leave Alaska.

"Obviously. He thinks we're there anyway. And you know how he is about people being on time for meals. Besides, Tamal's eating with us tonight, remember?"

"Fine," I said, dragging myself out of my chair. "What are we having?"

Abby shrugged. "Smelled like lasagna."

"Ooh, nice!"

I looked over at Uncle Joe, sitting there with his ears plugged and his eyes scrunched tight. He'd probably love some homemade lasagna after his weeks of soup and crackers and not much else. It was a shame he wasn't coming with us, really.

I bopped him on the arm, and he took his fingers out of his ears.

"We're, uh, we're . . . going in the fort now," I said. "There's a chance we'll be . . . making lasagna. Do you want some if we end up having extra?"

Uncle Joe struggled with himself for a moment, then nodded.

"Thanks, Maggie. That's thoughtful of you. I am getting pretty sick of soup. Though what I *really* miss up here is fresh green things. You wouldn't believe how much you can crave fruits and vegetables until you can't get them."

"I don't know about those," said Abby, "but we can definitely bring you lasagna. We'll set it outside the fort—"

"So you don't have to bother trying to fit in there with us," I finished.

Uncle Joe smiled. "Perfect," he said. "I'm glad you two kindred spirits are back together. You make a great team."

Abby threw an arm around my shoulder, catching me by surprise. "Oh, we're better than great, Joe," she said, squeezing. "We're the beluga-bawling best!"

My heart went all splashy. You could have knocked me over with a bubble net.

* * *

Five minutes later Abby and I and our freshly washed hands were sitting down to big plates of lasagna and green beans with Alex, the twins, and Tamal, who turned out to be short, muscly, and adorably shy.

"So, what kind of trouble did you two end up getting into

today?" asked Alex, passing me a dish and a serving spoon.

Abby and I broke into identical grins.

"That good, huh?" laughed Matt.

"Oh, no. No, it was a pretty normal day," Abby said airily. "You know, for us."

I kicked her foot under the table, then looked at the dish I was holding.

I looked down at my plate.

"Um, sorry," I said. "What am I supposed to do with this, exactly?"

Mark dropped his knife with a clatter. Alex looked shocked.

"You mean you've never put guacamole on your lasagna?"

"You poor thing!" said Matt.

"Abby!" said Mark, turning to his sister. "You never told her? And you call yourself a friend."

"That is enough out of all of you," Abby said, waving her fork. "Mags, just put it on your lasagna. It's the best thing ever, promise."

I did as she said and passed the bowl to Tamal, who leaned in.

"Thank you so much for asking," he whispered. "I didn't know what to do with it either." We clinked forks in solidarity.

"So it was just a normal day, then?" said Alex. "Well, I'll bet anything you two will make up for it with an epic time at Camp Pillow Fort tomorrow."

"Oh, wow," I said around a mouthful of guacamole and lasagna.

"See?!" said Abby and Mark together. I nodded.

"That is incredible," I said when I could speak again. "What do you call it? Guacasagna? Lasagnole?"

"Ew," said Mark. Abby snorted.

"We just call it good," said Alex.

"You really should come over for dinner more often, Maggie," Matt said. He reached past me for the salt, his arm muscles moving under his sleeve. "You've been missing out."

My stomach lurched like I'd just gone backward through the link to Uncle Joe's. Yup, I definitely had been.

After dinner Abby and I cleverly volunteered to wash the dishes so we could stash a secret container of leftovers in the back of the fridge, then piled into the living room with the others for back-to-back superhero movies.

When everyone started yawning, Tamal said good night, going around the room awkwardly shaking hands. "Your pillow fort–camp thing sounds fun," he said when he got to me. "I hope you have some really magical adventures with it this summer."

Abby started giggling and had to bury her face in a sofa pillow.

"Thank you," I said, kicking Abby under the blanket. "I think we might."

We all said good night again. Then the twins started another movie while Alex walked Tamal to his car, and Abby and I headed for bed.

"Are you staying over, Maggie?" asked Alex, poking his head around the bathroom door as Abby and I brushed our teeth.

"Does lasagna taste amazing with guacamole?" I mumbled around my toothbrush.

"Okay, I have absolutely no idea what you just said," said Alex, "but it sounded like yes. Sleep well, you two. Don't stay up too late."

Abby and I waited until the coast was clear, then launched a covert pajama-ops mission to retrieve the leftover lasagna from the fridge and deliver it to Fort Orpheus. It went off without a hitch, and after a quick stop on the way back to officially add Uncle Joe's fort to our map, we returned, triumphant, to Abby's bedroom.

"Man, what a day!" Abby said, bounding into bed.

I switched off the overhead light and settled into my spot in the entrance to Fort Comfy, the lamp glowing behind me. Another night or two and this would become routine.

"So," said Abby, crossing her arms behind her head, "Matt's getting pretty strong, isn't he?"

Warning! Warning! Cover blown! "Is he?" I said. "I guess. I mean—why would I know?"

Abby's smile definitely qualified as a smirk. "Just thought

I maybe saw you looking during dinner tonight is all."

I lobbed Creepy Frog at her. She caught him one-handed and tucked him behind her pillow.

"Don't worry, I won't tell. Night, Mags. Sweet dreams."

"G'night, you complete menace."

I flicked off the lamp and stretched out, smiling. Abby was right: it had been a day. I mean, Alaska! Alaska-Alaska-Alaska! That bay was seriously the most perfect place ever. A whole big playground of land and water with only one friendly grown-up in it. One friendly grown-up who specifically refused to find out what we were up to. It couldn't have been more perfect if I'd dreamed it up myself.

And it changed *everything*. Fort McForterson, Fort Comfy, and Fort Orpheus: that was our summer now. Sleepovers at Abby's, mornings in our forts, afternoons in Alaska escaping the heat, dinner with the twins, and all the very best games ever. Abby would come around. She'd realize soon that there was no point hanging on to her camp obsession when what we had was so much better. And I hadn't even gotten started yet. I was going to plan and direct and organize and make this the greatest summer vacation in history, just for her.

I closed my eyes, completely content, and was about to drift off when a soft, distinct thump sounded from behind the pillow that led to Fort McForterson.

I sat up, squinting blearily into the dark. Ugh. Not this again.

"Samson?" I whispered. "Is that you?"

Silence.

"Um, Uncle Joe?"

More silence.

". . . Mom?"

Nothing.

Frowning, I crawled through the link, switched on the light, and got the fright of my life. There was someone in the fort with me.

But it wasn't my mom. And it wasn't Uncle Joe.

It wasn't even Samson.

SEVEN

It was a girl, younger than me, with a baseball cap over her wavy black hair, sitting calmly in the center of the fort with her arms crossed, looking for all the world like she owned the place.

"Whoa!" I said. "What? Hi?"

"Maggie Hetzger," said the girl. It wasn't a question.

"Yes . . . ?" I'd never seen this girl before in my life. How did she know my name? And how long had she been here in my very own personal pillow fort? And hey . . . where had she even come from?

I started with the obvious question. "Who are you?"

"My name is Carolina," said the girl. She pronounced it the long way: Cah-roh-LEE-nuh. "I'm here to escort you to a meeting."

"A meeting?"

"A meeting. You need to come with me, Maggie Hetzger. Now."

We stared at each other. This was too weird. Thirty seconds ago I was half asleep in Fort Comfy, and now here I was being ordered by a perfect stranger to attend some sort of meeting in the middle of the night.

The secret-agent corner of my brain kicked slowly into gear, analyzing the situation. Hmm. Based on the available evidence, this might be some type of adventure.

"Well, we should go then," I said, deciding to roll with it. "I'll just get Abby."

Carolina shook her head. "Only the leader of your network is invited to the meeting."

The what? The leader of our *network*? If she meant our linked-up forts, then that meant me, but Abby definitely wouldn't want to miss this.

Except, said a quiet little voice inside me, *you missed out on camp. Why shouldn't Abby stay behind this time? She got her solo adventure. Why not you? Isn't it your turn to come back with stories to tell?*

"That's me," I said, swallowing hard. "I'm the leader." My stomach swooped—my first solo adventure!—but my heart gave a twinge. Abby hadn't left me behind on purpose; she'd had no choice. This wasn't quite the same. Then again, it didn't sound like I really had a choice either. Right?

"We know you are," said Carolina. "This way." She reached out and seized a blue-plaid wall pillow. It was one of the ones Abby had pulled down the day before, so I knew for a fact it led nowhere. I was just about to tell her so when Carolina yanked it aside, and a shining gold cushion appeared behind it.

I felt my jaw drop straight through the floor.

Carolina pushed the metallic cushion out of her way and crawled into the impossible link. I followed, dragging my jaw along with me . . .

. . . and staggered to my feet amid clamoring voices and a dazzling golden light inside a massive, gargantuan, *how-am-I-not-dreaming-this* pillow fort.

"Whaha—?" I said intelligently. "Whohow—?"

Whoa.

It was cavernous, at least five times bigger than the cafeteria at school. There was enough room to fly a helicopter. Carolina and I were at the outer edge, standing against a wall of mismatched pillows that curved away to either side, pillow after pillow after pillow circling the entire space. A bright patchwork bedsheet-and-blanket dome arced above our heads, rising to at least sixty feet high in the center, where a chandelier the size of a house shone like a sun made of fireworks, filling the whole place with that shimmering golden light.

I let out a breath I hadn't realized I was holding and looked down from the ceiling to the jam-packed floor beneath. And oh, that floor.

It was full to overflowing, a packed maze of sofas and pillow forts of every shape and size, with little paths and roads cutting between them. My eyes pinged around, trying to see everything at once. A fluorescent-teal sofa palace! A double-decker fort with a swing set! A row of minifridges! An avenue of bookshelves! An actual ball pit! And hey, it was the middle of the night—how were there kids *everywhere*?

Kids were chasing each other along the narrow paths, crawling in and out of the forts, pulling books off shelves, jumping on sofas, and clambering out from behind pillows, all as if this were the most normal thing in the world.

And just like that I was nervous. This was my first day of tennis lessons all over again. All these kids, talking, laughing, running, and I didn't know a single one. I didn't know my way around. I didn't know the rules. I didn't even know where I *was*.

And they didn't know me, either. No one here knew I was a master secret agent, or that I'd been running my own epic adventure games for years. No one knew I was cool.

"Keep up, Maggie Hetzger," called a voice, and I blinked back to my body. Carolina was heading off along the wall to my left.

I hurried to catch up, but flashes of sound coming from

behind the wall pillows kept hijacking my attention. If these pillows worked like the ones in Fort McForterson, then every one of them, stretching all the way around the room, could lead somewhere. That meant dozens and *dozens* of possible links. I slowed, trailing a hand across the changing fabrics, listening.

The roar of a waterfall boomed from behind a pillow covered in pink sequins; loud opera-style singing drifted through the next; chickens clucked around the edges of a thin green body pillow; and from an enormous cushion the size of a garage door came a steady bright clinking like a downpour of metal raindrops. I stopped and pressed an ear to it, my spy senses tingling.

"Maggie Hetzger!" yelled Carolina, sounding exasperated. She'd stepped away from the wall and was heading down a path directly onto the main floor. I jogged to catch up.

Kids looked around as I passed. Some smiled. Some waved. A few laughed. There sure were a lot of them. A girl carrying a trombone appeared from behind a bookcase, took one look at me, and broke into giggles. I flushed, my scalp prickling, and suddenly wished Abby were with me. She'd know what to do here. She'd stick by my side. She probably felt the exact same way when she got to camp all on her own. I did my best to summon my music, to walk with my head held high and the wind blowing through my hair. But it wasn't quite working.

Carolina led the way to the very center of the fort, where a round table sat on a platform beneath the gargantuan chandelier. The chandelier was stunning up close, all gleaming metal and golden lights, and decorated with bunches of . . . wait, kids?

There were kids up there, hanging thirty—no, fifty feet off the ground. I had to squint, but I could just make them out, geared up in black visors and climbing harnesses, crawling over the chandelier, dusting, polishing, and cleaning.

And hey, wait again! There were kids even higher up than that, dangling like window washers from the walls and ceiling, going at the curving blankets with needles and pins and thread.

Whoa. Times. Ten.

Beneath the chandelier four long banners hung all the way down to four chairs situated around the table. Four kids—two boys and two girls—were sitting motionless in the chairs, their hands flat on the table in front of them. They all wore matching silver sunglasses.

We climbed the steps and came to a halt. There was a long pause. The hubbub continued on the floor around us, but here on the platform everything was still.

"Welcome back, Carolina," said the girl sitting across from us finally. She looked a little older than me. She had silver hoops in her ears and a streak of purple in her short black ponytail. "Please introduce our guest." Apart from her lips the girl hadn't moved a muscle.

"Yes, ma'am," said Carolina formally. "Councilors, this is Maggie Hetzger. Maggie Hetzger"—she held out a hand—"this . . . is the Council."

I looked around and shivered. There was something deeply impressive about the way these kids were sitting there motionless, serene, bathed in that golden light. They looked like the statues in the Lost Temple of the Saber-Toothed Tiger, ancient and powerful. The one closest to me, a pink-cheeked boy in overalls who couldn't have been older than nine, had a clipboard and pen set neatly on the table in front of him.

"Um, hello, the Council," I said. What was the proper way to address a group like this? I needed more information. But I was determined to keep my cool. "So, what are you the council of, exactly?"

"Pillow forts, Maggie Hetzger," answered the girl with the ponytail. "We are the leaders and representatives of the four regional chapters of NAFAFA, the North American Founding and Allied Forts Alliance."

Oh. My. Creepy Frog. I felt my cool slip right off the platform.

I mean, sure, I was standing inside a palatial, impossible pillow fort, but *what*?!

"My name is Noriko," the girl continued. "Head of the

Council and Chancellor of the Forts of the Eastern Seaboard."
She raised a finger toward the banner above her head. It was
midnight blue and showed a silver ship sailing over a rolling
sea of pillows.

"This is Ben." Noriko nodded toward pink-cheeked Overall Boy. "Emperor of the Great Plains Sofa Circle." I looked
up to see a grass-green banner with a circle of wheat around
a plump yellow cushion.

"Next to him is Miesha, Queen of the United Southern
Gulf–Pacific Fortresses." Miesha had deep brown skin and a
pair of fancy tortoiseshell frames poking out from under her
silver sunglasses. Her banner was made up of three vertical
stripes—blue, green, blue—with a castle of orange pillows
rising in the center.

"And last is Murray, Captain of the Northern and Arctic
Alliance." Pale, sandy-haired Murray had a banner showing
a polar bear on a mound of white pillows under a pink-and-
purple sky.

I nodded, taking it all in, thankful for my years of spy
training as I burned their names and titles into my brain. I
was deep in unknown territory here; I needed every scrap of
intel I could get.

"I'm Maggie," I said, realizing they were all waiting for
me, "Vice Director of Camp Pillow Fort." Our name didn't
sound cool at all anymore.

I had a sudden horrifying thought and looked down.

Ugh. I was in my sleepy-dinosaur pajamas. That probably explained why all those kids grinned and laughed as I went by. "We, uh, don't have a banner yet," I finished awkwardly.

"Vice Director?" said Ben. He had a sharp, high voice. "The Alliance rules specifically state that only the very highest-ranking member of a group is permitted to solicit the Council under these circumstances."

My eyebrows bounced to the top of my forehead. What nine-year-old threw that kind of vocabulary around? And pronounced their consonants so precisely?

"That's true," said Carolina, stepping forward. "And I did my best, but I wasn't able to convince the Director of Camp Pillow Fort to come along."

"Why not?"

"Um, because he's a cat."

It was like someone flipped a switch. The atmosphere of regal mystery swirling around the group shattered as Miesha shouted "Ha!" and slapped the table; Murray squealed "Aww!" and put his hands to his cheeks; and Noriko began giggling, then laughing so hard she was practically crying.

Ben was the last to let his statue pose drop, but he wasn't smiling. "You broke!" he said angrily. "You were all supposed to stay in character! We were doing so well!"

"I'm sorry," said Murray, his palms still pressed to his face in delight. "But their leader's a kitty. A kitty!"

"Hey, we tried," said Miesha, stretching her shoulders

and beaming. "Good effort, Drama Committee. But now it's Snack Committee time!" She ducked under the table and reappeared with a giant plastic tub of popcorn and a jumbo carton of goldfish crackers.

Noriko was still half giggling. "Sorry! Sorry," she said, waving a hand at Ben. "I was just picturing Carolina sitting down and carefully explaining to this cat exactly why the Alliance rules require him to come to our mee-hee-ting . . . and the cat looking up at her—like—!" And she was back to rocking with laughter.

Carolina shrugged in a *Yeah, pretty much* gesture.

"Hey, this is serious!" said Ben. He jabbed a finger at his clipboard. "These rules are in place for a reason. I bet I could've got this director to come to the meeting."

"No, you couldn't," said Miesha around a mouthful of popcorn, "because having a cat in here would mean I'd be sneezing for the next three days." She turned to me. "You have to admit it's a weird choice, Maggie Hetzger. Do you have any other pets in Camp Pillow Fort?"

"Well, no, I don't— I mean—Samson's not mine." I stammered. I was completely thrown off by their abrupt change in tone. So, what? That first part was all an act? An act to impress or scare newcomers? What sort of game were these Council kids playing?

"Just because *someone's* got allergies . . . ," said Ben grumpily.

"He's just jealous because the rest of us have pets and he doesn't," Miesha informed me. "Do you want me to bring Sprinkles in again, Ben? Would that make you feel better?"

"All right, you two," said Noriko, pulling herself together. "We do have an actual meeting to get through here."

"Remember how fluffy he is?" Miesha continued.

"So fluffy!" said Murray. "The fluffiest there ever was!"

"That's right," said Miesha, throwing him a goldfish cracker. She looked around. "Hey, why am I the only member of the Snack Committee doing my job tonight?"

Ben groaned dramatically. "Because I did all the work on the Drama Committee, remember?"

"You are the Drama Committee," muttered Noriko. Murray giggled.

Ben glowered at them, but he ducked under the table like Miesha, returning with a tub of red licorice and a bag of marshmallows. "None of you deserve this," he grumbled, pulling the lid off the licorice.

Carolina nudged me as the others dove at the candy. "Sprinkles is Miesha's new puppy," she whispered. "She brought him in to visit last week, and Ben sort of fell in love. It's been pretty funny."

"And it's not even fair," Ben was saying as I tuned back in. "I can run the entire Great Plains Sofa Circle with an iron fist, but my mom thinks I'm not *mature* enough to have a simple pet."

"Well, everything you just said proves she's right," said Miesha reasonably, waving a piece of licorice at him. "Pets aren't simple, and you shouldn't need an iron fist to run your network."

Noriko raised her hand. "Hello? Seriously, we still have work to do."

"I run my network with a Ouija board," Murray said, to no one in particular.

Ben scowled at Miesha around his mouthful of marshmallows. "Just because you let *your* network run wild . . . ," he mumbled.

"Oh, you mean have fun? Thanks! My network *is* the most fun, and everyone knows it."

"Oh, give me a—"

"Enough!" said Noriko, standing up and banging on the table, the hoops in her ears swinging. "It's meeting time, people!" The other Council members fell silent. Ben was still glowering. Murray and Miesha grinned.

Noriko sat back down and turned her sunglasses on me. "So, yes, here we are—and Ben, seriously, we can let the leadership rule slide this one time." Ben shook his head and scribbled something on his clipboard. "You'll do fine for talking business, Maggie Hetzger. Welcome to the Hub."

"Thanks," I said. *Deep breath, Maggie, reclaim your cool.* "What's the Hub?"

"This place. Here. Where you are. The central pillow fort

for all of North America. This is where the regional networks meet up, the same way your fort is where all your links meet."

"It is?"

"Wait," said Ben, holding up a hand. "You hadn't figured that out yet? About your very own forts?"

"Um, no?"

"Wow." The corners of his mouth curled. "That should be obvious, even to a complete amateur like you."

Oof. What was this kid's problem? "Well, it's not," I said. "I have no idea what you're talking about."

"And that's totally okay," said Murray, lobbing a marshmallow at Ben's head.

Miesha leaned forward. "Maybe I can help, Maggie Hetzger. Try this. Close your eyes—no, really. Okay, take a deep breath. Now, imagine you're a dolphin. You are swimming through ancient seas. You are bathed in rainbows and starlight. Everything is beautiful. A purple unicorn swims by, leaving a trail of shimmering hearts. To your right is a pink-and-yellow panda. The midnight-blue ocean—"

"Miesha," I heard Noriko say.

I opened my eyes. Murray was shaking with silent laughter, and the others all had wide grins, even Carolina.

"Ha ha!" said Ben. "You got Lisa Franked!"

Wow. These kids were hilarious.

"Sorry, sorry," said Miesha. "It was just too perfect. For real now, though, Maggie Hetzger, picture your network for me. Please? Okay. So, where did the very first link from your original pillow fort lead, as far as you know?"

"To Abby's," I said promptly, because it had. I saw Noriko and Murray throw each other a look across the table, but Miesha kept going.

"Okay, good," she said. "And where did the second link go?"

"Uncle Joe's."

"Cool. Now, think about this: Do those other two forts connect to each other, without going through your fort on the way?"

I thought.

"The answer is no," said Ben. Murray shushed him.

"Well . . . they might," I said, frowning. "We haven't checked the pillows from the other forts yet. They could maybe link to—"

"They don't," Ben interrupted. "They really don't. Trust us—we're the experts here."

Murray and Miesha glared at him, but I was too distracted to care about Ben's rudeness. If what they were saying was true, and the forts in my network only linked up *through* Fort McForterson, then everything back home literally revolved around me. I was the center. I was the hub of Camp Pillow Fort. Huh. I liked that.

"Good, thank you, Miesha," said Noriko. "I think she's got it. And now that that's all clear, the main business we need to discuss, Maggie Hetzger, is you and your friend joining the National Alliance. Your network is still small, but it's developed unusually quickly, and it's time for you to step up and get with the pillow fort program. You've already come close to making some major mistakes—like oversharing with that uncle of yours, for a start—and we can't let you keep bumbling around like kindergartners anymore."

The thought suddenly flashed through my mind that maybe this was all a very bizarre dream, and any second now I would wake up in Fort Comfy feeling downright silly.

I pinched the inside of my wrist and winced. Nope, not a dream.

"Hang on," I said, as Noriko's speech hit home. "How could you know we almost said too much to Uncle Joe? You weren't even there." The answer smacked me in the face like a sofa cushion. "Wait—have you been spying on us?!"

"The Council and Alliance monitor all linked-fort activity," said Ben, patting his clipboard. "For your own protection, and for ours."

"And you were actually up there in Alaska the whole time?"

"We had NAFAFA agents listening from inside what you now call Fort Orpheus, yes," said Noriko. She held up a hand while I spluttered. "Look, our first duty here is to protect our own networks. That's what this entire meeting is about.

There's nothing more dangerous than a splinter group of uninitiated kids running amok and drawing the attention of the authorities."

"Authorities?" I said. Noriko was starting to sound a lot more like Ben. "What authorities?"

"Parents."

"And teachers."

"And lawyers."

They were all facing me. They looked deadly serious. Not even Murray was smiling now.

"Okay," I said. "Right. And you brought me here to . . ."

"To bring you into line," said Noriko. "We show you the way things work"—Ben gave a satisfied nod—"and teach you the rules. Then you either join us and start playing along, or we take . . . further steps."

"Further steps?" I repeated. That sounded like a threat. "What does that mean? And why do I have to follow your rules?"

Noriko leaned back in her chair. "How long have you and your friend been aware of the links, Maggie Hetzger?"

I thought. "A little over a day, I guess." Was that really all? It already felt like so much longer.

"And you're probably pretty excited about what you'll be able to do with them in a week or even a month from now, right?"

I nodded. If Abby and I weren't playing nightly galactic conquest games in the downtown library within two weeks, it wouldn't be my fault.

"Great," said Noriko. "Well, just for some perspective, I built my first linked fort and joined the Forts of the Eastern Seaboard five *years* ago. Everyone here has just a little more experience with this whole pillow fort world than you do, so you can trust us to know what's best."

"Five years?" I echoed. I was starting to feel like a parrot. "How do you even keep a pillow fort up for that long?"

Ben snorted, then choked on his mouthful of popcorn. Murray threw another marshmallow at him and gave me an encouraging smile.

"There are benefits to joining the Alliance, Maggie Hetzger," said Noriko. "A group like this doesn't exist for over three centuries without picking up a few tricks."

"Three centuries?!" It was official. I was a parrot.

Miesha raised her hand. "Hey, how about we just skip ahead to the tour? That way all these questions can get answered at once."

"Yes," said Noriko, pointing at Miesha. She looked around the table. "Who wants to give the tour and standard history lesson?"

"Ooh! Me!" Murray threw his hand in the air. "I'll do it!"

Miesha put a hand over her mouth to cover her smile.

Ben held up his pen. "Point of order. Newcomers aren't supposed to learn the history of NAFAFA until they've agreed to the entrance requirements, and this applicant still hasn't done that."

"Oh, I don't think a tour will hurt," said Noriko. "Besides, we need to talk about the you-know-what before this meeting can go any further. And since I think we can already tell which way Murray's going to vote "—Murray's forehead went pink—"the rest of us can stay here and talk about Maggie behind her back in peace."

Ben scowled, but he didn't object again as Murray got to his feet and led the way down the steps.

I followed, then glanced back as everyone around the table began talking at once. Were they really talking about me, like Noriko said? Why? And what were these "entrance requirements" I was supposed to agree to? They sounded downright ominous.

I turned and hurried after Murray, wondering exactly what sort of adventure I was getting myself into.

EIGHT

"Sorry about all this," said Murray, pointing to the workers on the ceiling as I caught up to him. "We don't usually do introductions on maintenance days, but you all are a bit of a special case."

"In what way?" I asked. But before he could answer there was a shout from the maze to our right.

"Murray! Murray! Murray-Murray-Murray!" A tall boy with shiny black hair launched himself out of a cluster of forts and wrapped Murray in an enormous hug. "It's been weeks! How's my favorite *capitaine*?"

"Oof! Bobby! How's it going?"

"Excellent!" said the kid. He locked Murray in another squeeze, then let him go and turned to me, beaming. "Who's your friend? Are you giving a tour? Which network is she in?"

"Her own," Murray said, catching his breath. "West coast!"

I had no idea what that meant, but the new boy looked very impressed. He held out a hand.

"Bobby," he said, dropping his voice low.

"Maggie," I said.

"Enchanté." Bobby gave a deep bow as we shook.

"Show-off," Murray said, grinning. He turned to me. "Bobby's in my network. He's from Montreal."

"Montreal by way of Taiwan," added Bobby, holding up a finger. He dropped his voice so deep he sounded like a movie preview. "Bobby is a global phenomenon."

"Nice," I said, smiling. "I'm from Seattle. By way of, um, Seattle."

"Nice!" Bobby said. "And this is your first visit to the Hub?" His already-beaming face lit up even more. "Hey, do you want to see the coolest thing ever in the history of the world?"

"Um, sure."

"Hooray! *Capitaine?*"

Murray gave a thumbs-up, and Bobby led us off the path to a boxy fort made of navy-blue sheets decorated with stars. We all ducked inside.

It was a neat, simple fort, with matching blue pillows lining the walls, a beanbag chair with a stack of comic books beside it, and twinkle lights strung around the ceiling. Bobby pulled down one of the pillows, set it aside, winked at me using his entire face, and disappeared through the link.

I crawled after him, feeling the soft carpet of the fort give way to the bouncy, smooshy squashiness of a deep pile of pillows. A very deep pile of pillows. It was almost pitch-black in the new fort, but as my arm sank up to the elbow I could tell this place would put Fort Comfy to shame.

"Where are we?" I whispered, trying to get my feet under me. My elbow knocked against something hard.

"Ouch," breathed Murray.

"Oop, sorry!" I reached out a hand to steady myself, and my fingers brushed a blanket wall, then stopped. Whoa. I pressed my whole hand to the fabric. There was a real wall behind it.

"Bobby," I said, reaching out with my other hand. Okay, there was a wall on my other side, too. "Where exactly"—my palm pressed flat just above my head—"are we?" Coolest thing in the history of the world or not, if we were boxed in a tiny crawl space or storage tank somewhere, I was getting out right now.

A faint light gleamed from the other end of the fort, showing Bobby's broad smile. Seriously, it was like he and Murray were competing for the World's Smiliest Tour Guide Award. "Come and see," he whispered. I squished my way through the pillow pile, keeping a firm mental grip on the exit, and heaved myself up beside him.

We were looking out an oval opening, just large enough for one of us to scramble through. Two rows of pale plasticky nubs curved around the inside, with thick rails of the same material arcing out in front on either side of— hold on—those were teeth, and those were tusks, and that meant . . . I pushed past Bobby and stuck my head through the gap.

We were inside a woolly mammoth. And the woolly mammoth was inside a museum.

Dim lights lit up glass display cases, dioramas, skeletons, and life-size furry models like the one we were snuggled up in. A fancy banner over the wall across from us read:

THE AGE OF THE MEGAFAUNA

Everything was still. We must have been the only ones in the entire museum. This was spectacular.

I craned my neck to see around the mammoth's side, and found myself face-to-face with an enormous stuffed moose. Its glass eyes glittered at me from beneath its sweeping antlers. My heart twinged. Abby would have loved to see this.

I crawled back inside the mammoth's belly.

"Isn't this the very greatest?" asked Bobby as my eyes readjusted to the gloom. "We came here on a class field trip when I was nine, and I wanted to know what was inside all the animals, so I just grabbed a tusk and climbed on in. I got in loads of trouble, but I'm glad I did it, because as soon as I joined the Northern Alliance, I was able to build a fort right inside Basil here. That's what I named him."

"Hi, Basil," I said, patting the wall beside me. "But how on earth did you get all these cushions and blankets and everything in here without getting caught?" It must have been a planning nightmare. This mammoth was literally stuffed with pillows.

"I camped out," said Bobby. "It was super fun, actually. I brought the starter blanket and pillows in a backpack and hid in the bathroom until everyone was gone for the night, then climbed in here just like I did when I was nine. Once Basil was linked in to my Northern Alliance fort, it was easy to bring the rest of the blankets and pillows in through the link."

Of course. That was brilliant. "So do you all run around the museum at night whenever you want?" I asked.

"Oh, yeah," Bobby said. "No one in the world knows this museum better than us." He sat up. "Hey, do you want a tour? I can show you the best exhibits right up close, and we can slide down the marble railings, and try on all the sweatshirts in the gift shop, and jump in the fountain if you want!"

"Thanks, Bobby," Murray said, "but we're already doing the new member tour here. And if we don't get a move on, I'll be in trouble for holding up the rest of the Council."

Bobby slumped dramatically against the pillow pile.

"Fiiiine," he said. "But I'm going to go splash in the

fountain for a bit. You two have fun!"

"Thanks for showing me Basil," I said.

"It was an honor meeting you," said Bobby. We shook hands, I got another full-face wink, and Murray and I headed back through the blue-star fort to the Hub.

"So," said Murray as we got to our feet. "That's Bobby."

"He's great!" I said. "Is everyone in your network like that?"

"Oh, no, there's only one Bobby," said Murray. "But my network *is* the most fun of the four. Everyone knows that."

Murray led the way back into the crowded maze of the floor, throwing out waves and greetings, and stopped at the far wall, where a tall red-and-gold tapestry hung between two mismatched pillows.

"What's this?" I asked, poking the fabric. The gold threads shimmered in the light from the chandelier. "How can a tapestry be a link?"

"It can't," said Murray. "The tapestry doors"—he spun in a circle and pointed to five other points along the wall—"are just regular doors. The rooms behind them are right here, part of the Hub."

"Wow," I said, craning my neck to look around at the massive space again. "So where exactly are we? A fort this size must be hidden inside a stadium or airport or something."

Murray beamed at me. "I asked that same question on my first tour," he said. "Don't worry—you'll find out in good time, eh? Come on." He pulled the tapestry aside and waved me through.

We stepped into a long, quiet hall lit with hanging lamps. It was super fancy. Gilded mirrors ran along each side, reflecting the polished wood floor and the walls and ceiling of pale sky-blue sheets. In front of each mirror was a short marble column with a different pillow on top. The whole place felt like an art museum, and I automatically put my hands behind my back as I leaned forward to read a plaque set under the first pillow, a dingy square with a cross-stitch pattern of daffodils.

NEW YORK, 1897.
ANNA ELEANOR ROOSEVELT.

"Okay, so this is where the tour actually starts," said Murray. He coughed, grinned, coughed again, and went on in a formal, tour-guide voice. "As Noriko told you, the story of NAFAFA goes back a very long way. This hall is where we preserve and display significant pillows from our pillow fort history, just as other networks around the world preserve theirs."

"Wait, there are other pillow fort groups around the world?" I said, standing up straight. "Seriously?"

"Of course. One Alliance for each continent except Antarctica. And they all keep their own records and histories.

Every pillow in *this* room is from a North American fort. Well, with one exception."

I whistled. This. Was. Awesome. Murray slowly led the way forward, giving me time to examine the different pillows on display: red velvet with white brocade; soft silver corduroy; worn black denim; rough burlap stuffed with straw; canvas painted with galloping horses.

"I recognize a lot of these names," I said, stopping at a plaque above a plain yellow square.

CALIFORNIA, 1939. NORMA JEANE MORTENSON,
LATER MARILYN MONROE.

"Yup," said Murray. "These pillows are all from former NAFAFA members who went on to do great things in the world. Their pillows are here to remind us of what we can do with our lives if we try. Everyone who joins NAFAFA dreams of having a pillow here someday."

"And that happens if you grow up and do something important?"

"Exactly. Not that you'll ever get to see it. Adults aren't allowed anywhere near the networks unless there's a life-or-death emergency, not even former members. We send a coded message and a nice plaque to people who get accepted, though, so they know. Look, here's someone who got in a bit more recently."

He led me over to a beautiful little pillow quilted in pink and blue roses.

Tennessee, 1955. Aretha Franklin.

"Hey, I know who that is," I said. "She's a singer. I like her."

"Everyone knows who she is," said Murray. "And she performed her first concert right here."

"In this hall?"

"In this hall."

I whistled again. "So this pillow is from . . ."

"Her first fort," said Murray. "When you age out of the network—which happens when you turn thirteen—you choose a pillow from your first fort and hand it in to the record keepers. It's stored in the pillow library, and once a year the Council goes through the pillows from exactly fifty years before and votes on whether any should get their own column."

"What happens if they get voted down?" I asked.

"Then they're released back into the wild," said Murray.

"The wild?"

"Junk shops, garage sales, that sort of thing."

I gazed up and down the hall. All these people, all these legends had started out as kids with pillow forts, just like me, and gone on to change the world. I looked down at the closest plaque. That could be my name someday. I could have a pillow here on my very own personal column. And years from now some future kid being led down this hall could stop to read my name and say, "Hey, I've heard of Maggie Hetzger!" and be amazed that I had been here too, right where they were standing.

I shook my head as the first curl of wind ran through my hair. I had to stay in the present, and there was something nagging at my secret-agent senses.

"What did you mean earlier?" I asked. "About every pillow here being from a North American fort except one. What's the one?"

"The next stop on our tour," said Murray. He led the way to the end of the hall, where a pillow made of green-and-gold velvet was set into the wall at floor level. It looked faded and fragile, and some big patches of fabric were missing.

"What's so special about this old thing?" I said. Murray shushed me and leaned down. Gently, reverently, he pulled the velvet pillow aside and crawled through the link.

I followed on my hands and knees—there was barely enough room to squeeze in—and immediately banged my head on something hard.

"Ouch!" I dropped flat, rubbing my skull. "Murray, what is this?"

"Easy!" said Murray. "Stop moving or you'll damage it. Just hold still until I'm out, then come through on your right."

I heard shuffling ahead of me, then footsteps. There was a whooshing noise, and a dim light appeared. I slithered awkwardly toward it and emerged, covered in dust, from under what turned out to be a dirty, broken-down sofa the same color as the ancient pillow.

"Whew!" I said, brushing myself off. "That was dramatic. Where are we now?"

We were in a small, old-fashioned room. Sunlight streamed through a delicate window high on the wall, lighting up the dust in the air from the velvet curtains Murray had just pulled open. The room looked as if it had once been fancy, with paneled-wood walls, a patterned-marble floor, and a heavy carved door opposite the window, but it had definitely seen better days.

So had the poor sofa. It was battered and worn, with a dust sheet dumped over one end and big chunks of fabric missing from the cushion running across the seat. The frame was sagging on the left side, which explained why I'd cracked my head crawling under it.

I looked around for any clues about our exact location, but there was only the sofa, the curtains, and a heavy-looking key hanging on a hook beside the door. I turned to Murray.

"Welcome, Maggie Hetzger," Murray said mysteriously,

"to where it all began." He spread his hands wide. "Welcome to the palace of Versailles."

I blinked. "The what of the what-now?"

"The palace. Of Versailles."

"*Vair-sigh*? That sounds kind of French."

"It *is* French." Murray reached up and pulled off his silver sunglasses. He looked much younger without them. His eyes were hazel with very pale lashes. "Weren't you wondering why the sun was already up?" He pointed to the window. "We're nine hours ahead of Seattle, Maggie Hetzger. We're in France."

NINE

I gaped at him.

"We are in France?" I pointed at the marble floor. "We are in a palace, in France, right now?"

"Yup," said Murray. "The world is full of wonders, eh?"

I probably shouldn't have been so shocked, seeing as I'd just linked up to Alaska a few hours before, but that was somewhere it was technically possible to drive to. Linking across the *ocean*? That was a whole other pile of pillows.

I stared around the dingy room. A palace? This? I guess it could have been. Not that I'd ever been in one before. Not outside my games, anyway.

"Okay, so why are we here?" I said, but just then a gaggle of grown-up voices rose on the other side of the door, headed our way. Murray's eyes went wide. He held a finger to his lips. I nodded.

The voices stopped right outside the room. One voice rose above the others, a woman speaking in superfast French. It sounded like she was explaining something, like a tour guide.

The woman switched to English with a heavy French accent, and my suspicions were confirmed.

"So, as before I will repeat for our guests who do not have French. This room is one of the favorite mysteries of Versailles. It is called le Petit Salon, or the Little Room. It was shut and locked nearly three hundred years ago in the time of Louis the Fifteenth and has never been opened since."

There was a murmur from the crowd, and the door handle wiggled as though the tour guide were trying it out. A burst of panic arced through me, but thankfully she was right about it being locked.

Someone in the group called out something I couldn't catch.

"No," said the woman, "no, there is no key. Every key in Versailles has been tried, and it is presumed that the key to this door must have been long ago lost."

My eyes jumped to the key hanging beside the door. I turned to Murray, my eyebrows raised, and pointed at it. He smiled.

"This room," the tour guide went on, "is believed to have been the favorite playroom of the young prince who would soon become the young king Louis the Fifteenth. Authorities on the palace history are assuring us there is nothing of value inside and that it is, in fact, likely to be empty. Of course, some are keeping other, more *exciting* theories. No one is knowing anything for certain, and with the door locked, the mystery must remain unknown as long as the palace of Versailles stands."

More murmurs from the crowd, some sounding amused, others puzzled. One distinctly American voice bawled out, "So why not just bust the door down?"

Several people tittered. The tour guide coughed meaningfully.

"The people of France, monsieur, are believing there are some mysteries that are worth preserving. But now, on!" She clapped her hands, fell back into rapid-fire French, and led the group of chattering grown-ups away.

I turned to Murray. "Louis the Fifteenth?"

"Louis the Fifteenth," said Murray. "He became king when he was only five, and this is where he played when he was allowed to be a kid. But what really makes it special is that this is the home of the first-ever linked pillow fort. This sofa"—he pointed—"in this room"—his voice dropped to a whisper—"is the center and source of it all."

He paused for effect. Dust motes spun and shimmered through a sunbeam above his head. I couldn't help feeling a little shiver.

"Cool," I said. "And you know that how, exactly?"

"Research," said Murray, returning to normal with a grin. "Our records aren't perfect, but we know that King Louis was nine when he got this sofa as a gift from an unknown ambassador. And before you ask, we don't know who. That part is still a total mystery.

"Louis liked the sofa, and he had it brought here to use in a pillow fort, because fun, right? Meanwhile his best friend—an eleven-year-old duchess named Yvette—was building a fort of her own under a sofa in the famous Hall of Mirrors. It sounds like they were playing Palaces, which was their version of playing House. Anyway, they swapped pillows as a sort of peace treaty, and next thing you know Louis was falling through a pillow right into Yvette's fort all the way across Versailles."

"Okay," I said, "wait." My head was starting to feel downright spinny with all these names and places. It was like sitting through Abby's talk about Camp Cantaloupe again. "Back up. You said you know all this from records. What records? Who has records of what this guy was doing as a kid all those years ago?"

"Museums, universities, top-secret government offices," said Murray, tapping them off on his fingers. "NAFAFA kids have snuck into most of them over the years. There are tons of historical mysteries that can only be explained by linked-up pillow forts, and we follow any threads we can looking for evidence. And treasure, too, sometimes.

"It was actually a former queen of Miesha's network who found the 'how it all began' story when she borrowed Louis's diary from the French national archives eighty years ago. She had to do some real secret-agent work to get in there, but it was worth it. Miesha's network runs the NAFAFA archives now, and they still have her notes if you ever want to read more about it."

"Oh, I've been doing that kind of secret-agent stuff for years," I said casually. Murray looked very impressed. "Well, you know, mostly in my head," I admitted. "But that still counts as practice."

"Well, once you're in NAFAFA you can give it a try for real!"

I nodded. I still had so many questions.

"So," I pushed on, "Louis linked from here to the Hall of Mirrors, and then what happened?"

"Right! So obviously he and Yvette were pretty excited about their discovery, and they went ahead and—"

"Tested the cucumber casserole out of it," I finished, nodding.

Murray laughed. "Ew! But yeah, exactly. And soon they figured out how tokens and everything worked, and they added more forts and formed the first real network. At first it was just within Versailles, but then they started linking to other palaces and castles around France, and things really got going. And that's how everything we have today began."

"Wow," I said. "But hang on. You used a word just now: *tokens*. What are tokens?"

"Tokens?" said Murray. "Really? They're the things—socks, books, you know, whatever—taken from a hub fort and put in new forts to make them linkable. The thing that has to stay there. The thing that lets them connect. Tokens."

My eyes slid out of focus as I digested what Murray was saying. Items from the hub fort, like Fort McForterson, being placed in other forts, like Fort Comfy, made those other forts linkable. So that was what had done it: the postcard I'd sent to Uncle Joe, the denim tassel scarf I'd given to Abby. Oof, it was a good thing I hadn't been handing out stuff left and right all summer! Who knows where Fort McForterson could've gotten linked to without me even knowing?

"So, just to be super, totally clear," I said, "you're saying if I take something—anything—from my pillow fort, which is a hub, and put it in another pillow fort, they'll link up? You're saying that's the whole trick?"

"Well, yeah," said Murray. "Did—did you really not know that yet?"

I shook my head.

"Wow." Murray rubbed the back of his neck. "That's *really* basic. Anyway, ta-da! Now you know how networks get made. But let me finish the story here. It's almost over."

I bowed like Bobby. Murray giggled.

"So," he continued, "little King Louis was happy with his

network of palace forts, and he had all sorts of adventures and got into all sorts of trouble, but before too long he grew up and had to start actually acting like a king. On the plus side he got to tell everyone what to do, but on the down side he was trapped in his palaces, since kings aren't ever allowed to go off and have adventures.

"Louis didn't like that; he wanted to see the world. So he sent pillows from this sofa out on all his fastest ships."

"To act as tokens," I said, feeling very smart.

"Right," said Murray.

"But wait, why whole pillows? Why not something simpler? You said they could be anything, right?"

"This was early days," said Murray. "The idea of linking across oceans was almost impossible to even imagine, so Louis sent pillows in case his normal everyday tokens like slippers and candles couldn't reach that far. His friends on the ships had orders to build pillow forts once they arrived, and when they did, Louis was suddenly able to travel anywhere he wanted. Well, anywhere he could send a ship with a pillow on it.

"He sent all the First Sofa's pillows out except the seat cushion here, and within a few years he was able to duck into his fort and run all around the globe while his guards and advisers thought he was just hanging out in here playing games."

"That's what Abby's dad always thinks we're doing!" I said.

Murray nodded. "It's a long, proud pillow fort tradition. Anyway, eventually it was all just too much for Louis to keep up with. He became a real grown-up, and being king was keeping him super busy, so he locked up the room to keep everything contained until he could figure out a time to come back. But he never did.

"The people in charge of his forts around the world kept them up just in case, and while everyone was looking the other way, their kids started playing in them instead.

"Of course, it turned out that kids were a whole lot better at running a pillow fort kingdom than grown-ups. It was the kids who figured out that each pillow was as powerful as the entire First Sofa itself, and that even a scrap of fabric from one of them could create a new hub. The pillows got divided into smaller and smaller scraps and pieces and spread around the globe, and soon the first major networks came together. Eventually the Continental Alliances and their Councils formed, and that is how," Murray concluded, back in his tour-guide voice, "we became the legendary society we are today."

He bowed.

I had to admit, I was deeply impressed. This was up there with the best spy adventure stories I'd ever imagined.

"So my fort," I said, "and Abby's fort, and Uncle Joe's, and your network and NAFAFA, all of it started right here, right where we're standing?" I eyed the place with a lot more respect than I had before. "And other kids from around the world come here too?"

Murray nodded. "Every Continental Alliance's hub has a link to this room. Sometimes we bump into each other. If there's ever a global catastrophe or crisis, everyone's supposed to meet here and try to solve it, I think."

"Wait, you think?"

"It's never been tried. When World War II began, some of the Councils met up, but we don't have records of them being able to do much more than protect this room."

"Protect it? From what?"

"Invaders. Grown-ups. Anyone who might want to break in. France was occupied during the war, and Versailles was full of foreign commanders and soldiers who were super curious about le Petit Salon and not as interested in preserving French mysteries as the locals."

"How did the kids protect it?" I asked, enthralled.

"Standing guard, mostly. There were kids stationed here twenty-four hours a day. Whenever anyone came near the door they would cry, or laugh, or clap their hands and sing counting games in off-key voices."

"And the invading soldiers would just run away?"

"Kids can be very creepy when they want to be," said Murray, putting his sunglasses back on.

I looked around the room, my imagination going into overdrive, and pictured myself standing guard all night in the darkness and dust. How boring. I would have run things much better if this were one of my games. Didn't kids back then have any sense of daring? "They really should've set a trap," I said. "And then lured the soldiers in one by one and captured them."

"Ah, well, they couldn't have done that."

"Why not? Not enough kids?"

"No, because they couldn't open the door," said Murray. "No one can. Not without smashing it down like your fellow American out there suggested."

I blinked. I looked at the door. I looked at the key hanging right beside it. I looked back at Murray.

I felt like there was some important point I was missing.

"But, okay," I said slowly. "We're inside the room, and the key's right there. . . ."

Murray gave me a long look from behind his sunglasses. "Unlock it, then," he said.

"What?"

"Unlock the door. Seriously. Maybe it's time."

Flecks of dust sparkled through the air between us.

"You mean it?" I said. "Really?"

"Really."

Slowly, with more than one glance back at Murray to see if he was kidding, I crossed to the door and lifted down the key. It was beautiful up close: a dull silver decorated with oak leaves around a radiating golden sun. It was surprisingly heavy.

"Go on," breathed Murray.

I took a deep, slow breath, thinking in a flash of the kind of summer I'd been having only a few days before: waiting by the mailbox for Abby's postcards, moping around in my lonely pillow fort, staring out at the world from my spot up on the roof . . . Things sure had changed. I exhaled hard and slipped the key into the lock that hadn't been opened in three hundred years. It fit.

I turned it.

The key didn't budge.

I tried harder.

Nothing.

I scrunched up my face and twisted my fingers back and forth until sweat broke out on my palms, but the lock refused to open. My hands fell to my sides.

"So, now you know," said Murray quietly.

"What's going on here?" I demanded. "What is this?"

"The real mystery of le Petit Salon," answered Murray. "That key's been there forever, but so far as we know it's never worked in that door."

"Well what's it for, then?"

"There are two theories," Murray said. "The first is that the key will only unlock the door for a certain person, a chosen one who will uncover the secrets of the origins of the First Sofa and bring about a golden age for the world of pillow forts."

I snorted. "Pass."

"I completely agree," said Murray. "It's way too *Sword in the Stone*. But some people really believe it. I know for a fact Ben comes in here every now and then to try the key again. He probably hopes he'll become the chosen one if he just keeps at it. I think he's wasting his time, though. I follow the second theory, which makes more sense but is much more frustrating."

"What is it?"

"That the key doesn't go to this door at all. That it goes to another lock entirely."

"Where?"

"That's the frustrating part," said Murray. He retrieved the key and hung it back on the wall. It swung gently, the edges gleaming in the light. "It's been three hundred years, and we still haven't got a clue."

TEN

Murray pulled the velvet curtains shut, then led the way back through the ancient sofa to the Hall of Records. The golden lights and shining mirrors were dazzling after the dusty sunbeams of le Petit Salon.

"Hang on a second," I said, swatting cobwebs off my pajamas as Murray reset the pillow. "How does a group that's only kids afford all this?"

"All what?"

"All this!" I flapped a hand at the mirrors and lamps and columns of glossy marble. "I get that it's been built up over hundreds of years, but this place must be pretty expensive to maintain."

"You're good at spotting problems, aren't you?" Murray said. "The answer's pretty simple. Have you ever sat down on a sofa with change in your pocket?"

"Yeah."

"And have you ever stood up and realized it was gone?"

"Yeah ..."

"And have you ever searched the cushions and not been able to find it?"

"Yeah!"

"Well, guess where a lot of it ends up."

The strange metallic clinking coming from behind the garage-door-size wall pillow danced through my mind.

"Here?"

"Here. I'll show you the collection fort later if there's time. Come on, we'd better get back."

"But how does—"

"Later, really. We have to go."

As we walked up the hall, familiar names on the plaques kept catching my eye: Frida Kahlo, Leonard Nimoy, Emily Dickinson, Alex Trebek.

"Alex Trebek?" I said, stopping at a blue-and-white pillow with Peter Rabbit hopping across it.

Murray looked over. "What about him?"

"Isn't he the one from that TV show?"

"Yup. He came through here when he was our age, and now he's one of the most famous Canadians ever."

"Alex Trebek is Canadian?"

"A lot of people are, Maggie." Murray started up the hall again. "So now you see," he said, returning to his tour-guide voice, "why it's so important we make sure new members deserve to join our group. NAFAFA is one of the most exclusive secret societies in the world, and you'll need to prove that you and your network are worthy to join."

"How do we prove it?" I asked as we pushed past the tapestry into the Hub.

Murray attempted a Bobby-wink over his shoulder.

"That's for Noriko to tell you."

We returned to the platform, where Noriko, Miesha, and Ben stood around the table, studying a large sheet of paper spread open between them. Noriko jumped and rolled it up hastily as we approached, but not before I thought I recognized the lumpy shape sketched across it.

"Wait, wasn't that Camp Pillow Fort?" I said. "Is that a map of our network?"

Three pairs of silver sunglasses turned in my direction. Murray nudged me and shook his head. I ignored him.

"It looked funny," I pressed on. "We've got a map too, and the shape the forts make when you draw them together is different. Yours had extra lumps. Can I see it again?"

Ben turned to Miesha, who turned to Noriko.

"Let's deal with our business first," she said. "We can talk about other issues later."

They all sat down, and Murray directed me to a new chair

tucked beside his. I scooched in. It felt right, sitting at the table with the other kids in charge. They might have had more experience, but I ran a network too, just like they did. When it came down to it, we were equals.

Noriko folded her hands. "So, Maggie Hetzger," she said. "If Murray has done his job, you should now have some idea what NAFAFA is all about. This is a historic organization with a grand history, and it is our duty to protect its strength and integrity for the fort builders who will come after us. They, after all, will be our judges, and we cannot let them down."

She sounded exactly like Murray doing his tour-guide voice. The other Council members were nodding.

"As I said before, your network has come together unusually quickly. Now it's time to make things official. So as NAFAFA applicants, you and the other members of Camp Pillow Fort are hereby forbidden from: one, forging new links; two, adding new forts; and three, passing linked-fort information to a single other person until your admission into the Alliance has been approved."

I felt my mouth fall open. So much for being equals. "What?!" I said. "But Camp Pillow Fort is mine—I mean, mine and Abby's. What makes you think you can tell us what to do with our own personal network?"

"Hey, easy," said Miesha. "This is how it's been done for centuries. And it's for your own good. You wouldn't be able to cope with more links right now, anyway."

"We totally could!"

"No, you totally couldn't." Miesha shook her head, smiling. "I know you think that, but trust me, I manage *sixty-four* links in my network. That's on top of school and friends and everything else—"

"Like Sprinkles the puppy," piped up Murray.

"—like Sprinkles the puppy," continued Miesha. "And it's a ton of work, even with four years of experience. It's really better to start slow."

"Miesha's correct," Ben said. "You're hopelessly behind everyone here, so you should just do as you're told. It's not like you have a choice, anyway. Our rules must be followed."

I scowled at him, and at his overalls. This kid sure was good at getting under my skin. Why was he always so rude? And for that matter, what was a little boy like him doing on the Council in the first place?

"Okay, how old are you anyway, Ben?" I asked impulsively. "Aren't you kind of young to be sitting at the big kids' table?"

Miesha threw back her head and laughed. Murray bopped me under the table with his foot. Ben smiled. It wasn't particularly friendly.

"I'm nine," he said. "I'm the youngest Council member ever. And someday I'll be the youngest head of Council, too."

"Maybe, buddy, maybe," said Noriko. She turned to me. "Ben's a bit of a special case."

"If you say so," I said. "But hey, Murray said my group was a special case too. Does that mean I get some say about the rules?"

There were three seconds of silence, then . . .

"Way to give it away, Murray!"

"We agreed not to say anything!"

"That is completely against regulations!" Ben was on his feet, waving his clipboard. "You could be kicked off the Council for that."

"Hey, hey, hey," said Murray, holding up his hands and looking alarmed. "Easy with the regulations, eh? All I said was their group is a special case. I didn't give away anything important."

"Telling them they're a special case is plenty!" said Ben. He rounded on Noriko. "What are you going to do about this?"

Noriko tilted her head, considering, then shrugged. "Nothing. If Murray only mentioned the situation to Maggie Hetzger, I don't think it's a disciplinary matter."

"Thank you," said Murray. "Ben, sit down."

"This is completely ridiculous!" Ben yelled, plonking down in his chair. "I move for a special vote to throw Murray and Noriko off the Council!"

"Now who's being ridiculous?" said Noriko.

"You are!" Ben sounded like he was on the verge of a tantrum.

"Hey, don't talk to Noriko like that," said Miesha. "Especially not in front of guests."

"Maggie Hetzger is much more than a guest," objected Murray.

Suddenly everyone was talking at once, waving their hands and pointing dramatically across the table. It was turning into a full-blown ruckus when one of the bulbs in the chandelier above us blew with a sharp pinging pop.

"Bulb!" cried a muffled voice from the maintenance crew over our heads. A tiny shower of glass shards tinkled down behind Ben's chair.

The Council members all looked up. "Bulb!" they shouted in unison. The background hum of voices filling the Hub stopped abruptly.

In the silence Noriko raised her hands over her head and clapped three times. I glanced around. Every eye in the place was fixed on the chandelier.

"WAY TO GO, KID!" yelled every last person in the Hub except for me. "KEEP IT UP! HAAA-AAAVE FUN!"

Noriko clapped again, and the talk and chatter returned as everyone went back to what they were doing.

"So," said Noriko, turning to me, "as I was saying, in addition to freezing your network—"

"Wait, wait, wait," I said. "What just happened?"

Noriko frowned. "Please don't interrupt, Maggie Hetzger. We've had enough of that for one day."

"But what was that chant thing you all just did?"

"Oh, that. There's a tradition that every time a bulb burns out in the NAFAFA chandelier, a kid somewhere in North America has just built their first pillow fort. That means they might discover linking and end up here someday, so we mark the moment to wish them well."

I looked up at the chandelier. "Really?" That was pretty out-there, even for me.

"Yes, really," said Miesha. "Now will everyone please let Noriko give the instructions so we can get this meeting over with?"

"Thank you, Miesha!" said Noriko. "So, Maggie Hetzger. In addition to freezing Camp Pillow Fort, there is one important thing you need to do before you and your network can be accepted as members of NAFAFA: you must use your forts"—she paused dramatically, her sunglasses glinting in the golden light—"to perform a good deed."

I blinked.

"I'm sorry?"

"You must use your forts to perform a good deed," repeated Noriko. "A very good deed. And you have exactly three days to do it."

I stared at Noriko for a full five seconds before I realized she must be joking. Weird lighting-fixture traditions or not, these just didn't seem like the sort of kids who would run their club like a fairy tale. I burst out laughing.

"Ha!" I said. "That's hilarious. What, are we supposed to give a wandering old woman shelter for the night? Or defeat the evil adviser to the empress? Or rescue a cursed prince who's been turned into a washing machine that makes everything washed in it turn to gold, and the only way to save him is to track down his matching dryer and decipher the counterspell written in code on the lint trap?" I made a mental note to actually remember that one for later. "I mean, you're totally kidding, right?"

Four silent faces told me they weren't.

Oh, cucumber casserole. Way to go, Maggie.

"Wow, okay." I tugged at my pajamas. "So, um, what do you want us to do?"

"That's up to you and your network," said Noriko. "Coming up with a quality good deed is part of the test. We want to know you can think of others and use the powers of the forts for good. We'll judge your efforts and vote, and if we approve, you'll be in."

"And if you don't approve?" I asked. "What happens then?"

"If you don't meet our expectations, then you are officially declared a rogue network and we attack and shut you down."

She spoke so calmly, so matter-of-factly, that I almost missed it.

"Wait, *attack*?!" I said as the news reached my brain. "What sort of attack?"

"Parental," said Noriko, "the most effective kind. Break our rules or fail to meet our expectations and we'll let kids loose in your house. Kids who will eat your food, mark up your floors, track dirt on your carpets, leave the cap off the toothpaste, unmake your bed, hide your family's favorite things in your fort, and generally do everything they can to make sure you get in trouble. There's no way to prove it wasn't you, and nine times out of ten it results in the demolition of the fort and loss of fort-building privileges forever."

I stared at her. The fairy tale had become a gangster movie. I looked over at Murray, but his eyes were fixed on the table. "That is . . . that's horrible," I said. "Do I even want to know what you do the one time out of ten it doesn't work?"

"In those cases we remove the causal element ourselves," said Ben. His unfriendly smile was back.

"The casual what-now?"

"The *cau-sal el-e-ment*," he said, tapping out each syllable on his clipboard. "The thing with a scrap of the First Sofa in it that makes your network work. For you that means the patchwork scarf."

"My scarf?" I said, appalled. "But Abby made that for me. You can't just steal my things!"

"We know," said Miesha. "That's why removing the causal element is only used as a last resort. We don't really want to take someone else's things, but if it's a choice between that and endangering the entire Alliance, well, we kind of have to."

"Exactly." Noriko nodded. "And Ben is correct, Maggie Hetzger. You don't have a choice about the good-deed test. If you refuse to take it, we'll declare you a rogue network and shut you down right here. The only way you can keep your links is to do what we say and pass the test. Maybe that seems unfair now, but the benefits of NAFAFA membership outweigh any unfairness by a thousand to one. In the end, we're doing you a huge favor by asking you to join."

I looked around at them. After that tour I'd been ready to sign up in a heartbeat so Abby and I could go all real-life-secret-agent on those museums and palaces and secret archives. But in just the last few minutes I'd been insulted, ordered around, and threatened, and I wasn't totally sold on the idea of merging my very own personal pillow fort network with a group of kids like that.

Then again, if it came down to either joining NAFAFA or losing the links forever, well, Noriko was right—I really didn't have a choice. Abby would always be next door, but losing Uncle Joe and Alaska? Losing all that space and freedom when we'd only just found our way there? That was definitely not an option.

"It looks like you've got a lot to think about," said Noriko, eyeing me. "Why don't we assume for now that you're agreeing to the test, and you can go home and talk it over with your network? It's not really such a big deal, doing one good deed."

"Talk it over with my network," I said, "right." What would Abby say to all this? Old Abby would have loved the woolly mammoths and famous pillows and palace doors and missing keys, but what if New Abby didn't? Or hey, even worse—

"What do I do if Abby doesn't believe me?" I said.

Murray tilted his head. "Why wouldn't she? You're best friends, right?"

"Obviously," I said. "But she's not exactly the same as she was before she went away to camp. I don't know if I can guarantee I'll be able to convince her." It felt weird to be talking about it with them, but there was too much at stake here not to bring up potential problems while I had the chance.

"Don't worry," said Miesha. "You'll be fine. I had the same trouble with some friends back when I joined. We'll help if you need it."

Noriko got to her feet, and everyone else did the same. It looked like the meeting was over.

"Good-bye, Maggie Hetzger," Noriko said, reaching across the table and shaking my hand. "Thanks for coming. Carolina will take you home."

I jumped as Carolina appeared at my elbow, then I shook hands with Miesha, who smiled encouragingly, and Murray, who turned pink again. Ben hugged his clipboard to his chest and gave me a curt nod.

Carolina and I set off down the steps, but I only made it a few feet before I stopped and turned back, the one big question I'd been dying to ask since the beginning tumbling out before I could stop myself.

"Hey, so why exactly are you all wearing silver sunglasses?"

Everyone froze. Out of the corner of my eye I saw Carolina put a hand over her mouth. There was a very uncomfortable silence.

"Because, Maggie Hetzger," said Noriko, drawing herself up to her full height, "we . . . are the Council."

And she waved me away.

ELEVEN

I lay awake for hours after my visit to the NAFAFA Hub, going over every unbelievable detail in my mind and trying to figure out what exactly I should do.

The trouble was, those Council kids had made it crystal clear I didn't actually have a choice. It was pass their test or lose the links forever, and that was that.

Well, if I had to join their club, at the very least I could set up rock-solid boundaries. Camp Pillow Fort was a network of two, and it was going to stay that way. The rest of them could have sixty-four links and all the kids they wanted, but Abby and I only needed each other.

I stared into the darkness of Fort Comfy, trying to imagine everything that could possibly go wrong in advance; and when I finally did fall asleep, my dreams were full of locked doors, dusty halls, broken mirrors, and creepy children singing songs about licorice.

So it was a rough start to the morning when Abby crowded into the fort, tickled me awake, and demanded I do my duty as vice director and lead a proper morning roll call.

"Director Saa-aa-mson," I said, losing a battle with a yawn. I'd barely gotten any sleep, and I felt all bleary and blotchy next to Abby, who was unfairly bright eyed and shiny haired and raring to get on with the day.

"Probably napping on the back porch," said Abby. "So, absent!"

"Hernandez, Abby."

"Hesitant!" Abby punched the air.

"And He-etzger, Magg-ieee." Another yawn. "Pleasant."

Abby poked me in the ribs. "Is that the best you can do?"

I propped myself up on one elbow and rubbed the sleep out of my eyes. "I've got something to tell you. . . ."

"Cool, but first," said Abby, "can we make it a plan to come up with a camp dance today? It was one of the very best parts about Camp Cantaloupe, and I think we've been overlooking it."

"If you want," I said. "But you really, really need to hear this. . . ."

I told her every detail of my adventure, from the Hub kids to the First Sofa to the Council's ultimatum. Abby listened, her eyebrows inching higher with every word.

". . . so we actually have a lot to do today," I concluded, "because this is Day One, and if we don't get this done by Day Three, we'll lose the links for good."

Abby stared at me. "Wow, Maggles. I am *impressed.*"

"Huh?"

"You must have been awake all night making that up!"

"What?! No, I didn't—"

"We should still focus on our summer camp setup, since we've put so much time into it, but we could work this new game in around the sides, maybe. Who did you want to pretend to be the Council?"

"Hello," I said, waving at her. "This isn't a joke. This isn't a game. This is real, it's happening, and we need to get started."

"Dude, it's okay," said Abby. "You don't have to try so hard. I'll play along."

"No, I *do* have to try so hard because you're still not getting it." I sat up and looked her dead in the eyes. "This is not a game. I'm—not—kidding."

Abby blinked, the smile sliding from her face. "You're not?"

"Not even a little."

"But Mags, come on. You have to be. I mean, all that secret-room, mysterious-key stuff, it's totally *you*. It's the exact kind of story you would stay awake all night dreaming up."

"I know, but I swear I didn't," I said. "Look, I'm the one who went. I know what happened and you don't. You're in no position to argue here."

"Well"—Abby looked around the fort—"do you at least have some proof, or something? Like a souvenir, or a mark on a pillow?"

Shoot. I'd been hoping she wouldn't ask that. "No," I admitted. "I don't. Carolina came in through the blue-plaid pillow in my fort, but it doesn't lead anywhere now; I checked as soon as she brought me back."

"Huh." Abby crawled past me through the link to Fort McForterson. I followed, watching as she pulled the pillow free, studied both sides carefully, and tapped the chair legs behind it. It all looked so mundane and normal in the morning light.

"You're absolutely *sure* it was this one?"

"Positive. You'd remember if it happened to you."

She sat back, chewing her lip. "Mags, I'm sorry. I mean, without any proof, and it's so much like one of your— Just—I don't know." Her eyes flicked to my face, then away. "I'm, uh, gonna go brush my teeth." She headed back to her fort.

I slumped against the side of the sofa. New Abby was out in full force.

I was deciding the best way to tell her exactly how moose

headed she was being when there was a shout from Fort Comfy.

"Look!" Abby yelled, bursting back through the link. "Look-look-look-look!" She held out a large silver envelope. "It's got my name on it! I swear, this was not there when we crawled through a second ago."

"What's inside?" I asked.

Abby pulled out a square of heavy paper and scanned it, her eyes going so wide she looked like a cartoon character.

"Well?" I demanded. "What's it say?!"

"It says, 'Dear Abby Hernandez, Maggie Hetzger is telling the truth. Signed, The Council of NAFAFA.'"

There was a very satisfying silence.

"But how," Abby said, shaking the envelope, "how did they get this in my fort?"

"No idea." I was having the hardest time not grinning from ear to ear. It was a nice feeling being right. "But Noriko did say they'd help if I had trouble convincing you. This must be their way of doing it."

"Unbelievable." Abby stared down at the note, then looked up. "Wait—so does that mean they can hear everything we're saying?"

"It looks like it. They told me they 'monitor all linked-fort activity.' But it's probably way too late to worry about that now."

"This is just so bizarre. I mean, this changes everything."

"You have no idea."

"Will you tell me the whole thing again, Mags? From the start? I want to make sure I really understand what's going on. I promise I'll pay attention this time."

"Oh, thanks so much," I said. "Okay . . ."

I repeated the story, making sure to include every tiny detail, and Abby listened closely.

"So there was a piece of the First Sofa in that quilt I used to make your scarf?" she said when I finished. "That is so cool. I basically started this whole thing!"

"Well, the fact that I built a pillow fort might have helped some."

"But it took my scarf to make the fort link."

"By our powers combined, then."

"And so now we have three days to pull off a good deed or it's all over?"

"Yup."

"No problem!" Abby slapped the note against her palm. "Getting in will be easy. I mean, it's *us*, and then we'll have so many more people to hang out with. It'll be just like back at camp!"

My happiness at finally convincing her I was telling the truth vanished with a pop.

Whoa. My whole reason for joining NAFAFA was so we could save our links and get access to all those new ones for better-than-ever games. Games that needed a Maggie and an Abby, and no one else. Sure, I would have to go to Council meetings sometimes, and there was probably some sort of newsletter I'd have to read, but I could manage all that and still have the time of my life with my best friend.

Only it sounded like Abby wanted to join NAFAFA so she could hang out with new kids, just like she did at Camp Cantaloupe. That meant the sooner we did our good deed and joined, the sooner she could dive into that kid-packed maze on the floor of the Hub. It was completely unfair. I'd only just gotten Abby back! I wasn't ready to start sharing her again. Why couldn't things just be the way they used to be?

Good thing I still had three whole days to think of a solution.

"So hey, let's do this!" said Abby. "I'm guessing you were up all night and have, like, seventeen good deeds planned out already, right?"

I blinked. She was right. Old Maggie would have had this mission drawn up, scripted, and set to music by now; but I hadn't even thought once about the good-deed part of the quest.

"Let's brainstorm ideas together," I said, playing for time. "We've got days to work with here. There's no rush."

"Oh, no," said Abby, "I think we should get it—" But she cut off as a loud knocking came through from Fort Comfy.

"Oh, whale poop!" Abby said, her wide eyes mirroring mine. We dove back through the link.

"There you are," said Alex as we scrambled out into Abby's bedroom. "What took you so long? I've been knocking for half a minute."

"Uhh," I said.

"Umm," said Abby.

"Well, never mind," said Alex. "Maggie, your mom called."

"Who?" I said, still slightly panicked.

Alex smiled. "Your mom. The lady who lives next door. She'd like you to come home after breakfast. She wants to check in about a few things before she leaves for work."

"Oh, okay." I was surprised—it wasn't like my mom to call and check on me. Then I remembered she hadn't actually seen me in almost two days.

Abby and I got dressed while Alex made scrambled eggs and orange juice, and after helping with the dishes we headed over to my place.

My mom was folding laundry at the dining-room table.

"Hi, sweetie," she said, flapping out a pair of jeans as we came in. "You forgot to leave a note last night."

"Sorry," I said. "I was only next door."

"I know—that's why I called you there. Hi, Abby. Nice braid."

"Thanks, Ms. Hetzger!"

"How was your time at camp?"

"It was great!" said Abby. "I wish Maggie could have gone."

I took advantage of the moment to give my mom a pointed look, but she had a towel tucked under her chin and didn't see.

"Glad to hear it," she said. "Maggie, I'm leaving for work pretty soon here. I picked up groceries last night, so there's plenty of food in the fridge. Make sure you eat a salad or something healthy for lunch, okay?"

"Okay. Will you be around later?" I asked. It was great having all this parent-free time to spend with Abby, but I didn't mind my mom being around sometimes.

My mom shook her head. "We're stretched thin on staffing this week, so I'm covering shifts where I can." She noticed my expression. "I'm sorry, but you know I can't always be around just because you want me to be. Remember, you're almost in middle school now, and I'm proud of how mature and responsible you are at taking care of yourself and our home. And speaking of, I need you to give the whole house a good clean this afternoon."

I failed to suppress a groan.

"Hey, no need for that," said my mom. "We talked about this. Chores are a part of life." She glanced at her wrist. "See?

I'm giving up taking a shower so I can get our laundry folded before I head back out to work. I don't think asking you to take a few hours out of your vacation to tidy up is too much to ask." She began tugging at a tangle of T-shirts.

"Ms. Hetzger?" said Abby, raising her hand. "We can do it."

"What?" my mom and I said together.

"We can fold the rest of the laundry," said Abby. "That way you'll have time for a shower."

My mom stared at her; then her face relaxed into a surprised smile. "Thank you, Abby," she said. "I'll take you up on that. Pants creased at the seams, please, and socks folded, not rolled." She headed for the hall, then stopped in the doorway and turned back. "By the way, do you two have a radio or something hidden in that pillow fort?"

"Um, no," I said, with half a glance at Abby. Why was my mom asking questions about the fort?

"I could have sworn I heard noises and talking in there after I hung up the phone with Alex."

"Weird," I said, now looking everywhere but at Abby. I picked up a dishcloth and started folding. "You must have imagined it. There's nothing in there that makes sounds."

My mom leaned against the doorframe. "Yeah, I didn't see anything when I went in, but I thought I'd ask."

My head shot up. "You went in my pillow fort?"

"I've been in there before," she said. "It's not exactly private property, is it? Although, speaking of private property, it was nice to not see any of my things hidden in there this time."

"But—but you can't just—" I spluttered.

"I think today is actually the perfect time to take it down, as long as you're cleaning the house. You haven't even been in there since Abby got home, and I'd like to have the living room back to normal."

My mouth was opening and closing like a fish, but no words were coming out.

"We can't take it down for a bit, Ms. Hetzger," said Abby quickly. "See, we built one at my place, too, and we're playing this, uh, summer camp game with them, since Maggie couldn't go to the real one."

"Oh." My mom looked like she wanted to argue, but her eyes flicked to me. The reminder of the Camp Cantaloupe paperwork mix-up seemed to be holding her back. "Well, all right. But take that fort down soon, okay?"

"Just don't go in there again," I blurted out. Really, I had enough to deal with without her getting involved.

My mom looked a little hurt. "Hey, I'm the parent here, Maggie." She glanced at her watch. "And I'm about to set a record for world's shortest shower." Her footsteps thudded down the hall as Abby and I turned to the mountain of laundry.

"Why did you say we would fold all this?" I asked, launching my dish towel back into the heap.

For some reason Abby was grinning. "Isn't it obvious?" she said. "We're doing a good deed! We should be on the lookout for good deeds all the time from now on. Oh, and you're welcome by the way for saving your fort."

I looked over the table. "A good deed? Really? This seems more like a favor to me. I don't know if non-fort-related laundry counts."

"Only one way to find out," said Abby, shrugging.

"Okay, fine," I said. "Just warn me next time you're gonna go all thoughtful and helpful, all right? You made me look selfish in front of my mom."

Abby snort-laughed. "You were kinda doing okay at that on your own."

I threw a pair of folded socks at her.

Ten minutes later my mom flew by and out the door, and ten minutes after that we had all the laundry folded and stacked into neat piles.

"Good deed!" said Abby, raising both arms over her head. She looked around the room. "Do you think they heard me?"

"How would I know?" I grumbled. The day wasn't exactly going my way. Why was everybody else trying to run things?

"Better safe than sorry," said Abby. She went over to the fort and stuck her head in the entrance. "Good deed!"

she yelled again. "Laundry folded so Maggie's mom could shower before work. Good deed!"

I gave her a look as she came back in.

"Oh, stop being Grumpy Mags," said Abby, poking me on the shoulder. "It doesn't suit you. Now, what's next? More good deeds, or cleaning first?"

"We should probably clean," I said reluctantly. "Then let's go hang out with Uncle Joe. We can brainstorm good-deed ideas up there."

"Ooh, good call," said Abby. "Maybe Joe can—" She stopped. Her eyes went out of focus. She spun and looked at the fort, then back at me. "Mags!" she said, slapping at my arm. "Mags-Mags-Mags-Mags!"

"What? Ow! Why do you do that? I'm right here!"

"I've got it! Another good deed! One we can do right now!"

"Great," I said, fending her off. "What?"

"Greens."

"Greens?"

"Greens!"

"Are you speaking in code right now?"

"No, I mean greens! Like vegetables. And fruit, too, I guess. But greens! For your uncle Joe. Remember how he said he was craving fresh stuff because he couldn't get any up in Alaska?"

"Yeah..."

"So let's make him a big salad for lunch and bring it to him! Your mom said she got plenty of groceries."

"You want to bring a salad," I said slowly, "for lunch, to Alaska. That's your good deed idea."

"Totally!" Abby said. She sighed at the look on my face. "Admit it, Grumpy McGrumperton, it's great!"

I shook my head, but my mouth twitched into a smile. There was no way it would work, but it was better than cleaning, and it would give me more time to figure out how to keep the links without losing Abby to all these new kids.

"Fine," I said. "But you're carrying it up through that spinny-whirly link."

"Deal!" said Abby. She looped her arm through mine and steered me into the kitchen. "Come on, time to make the most epic salad the world has ever seen!"

TWELVE

"Knock, knock," I called as we crawled out of Fort Orpheus an hour later. "Hello? Uncle Joe?"

No reply. It looked like he wasn't in.

"He's probably out on the water," Abby said. "Sweet, that'll make this more of a surprise."

We brought our thoughtful good-deed salad into the kitchen and went to look out the windows. Things had changed up in Alaska. Instead of a shiny blue sky, a solid bank of gray clouds loomed from one side of the horizon to the other. It was bright and warm in the cabin, but for some reason the sight of that sky made me shiver.

"Look, there he is," said Abby, pointing down to the water's edge. She squinted, then grabbed my arm. "Hey, I think he's hurt!"

I looked where she was pointing. Uncle Joe was limping slowly over the rocks, headed our way.

We threw on coats from the closet and ran to meet him.

Outside, the wind was blowing hard, making little white-caps ripple over the waves. Maybe a storm was coming. Thank goodness we'd shown up when we had. It hadn't really occurred to me before how very, very alone Uncle Joe was up here.

He caught sight of us racing toward him and raised a hand, smiling.

"Here comes the cavalry," he called as we approached. "Don't worry, don't worry, I think I'm okay."

Abby and I pressed around him, offering hands and asking what had happened. He rested an arm on my shoulder, steadying himself as we inched back to the cabin.

"Just a twisted ankle," he said. "I slipped getting out of the boat and went down like a giraffe on ice. Probably looked pretty funny, to tell you the truth."

"It's not funny at all!" I insisted. "What if you were really hurt? What if the boat rolled over and crushed your foot? What if you broke your leg and got pulled into the water by the tide? You need to be more careful!"

Uncle Joe grinned. "You sound just like your mom. She hasn't stopped worrying about me since the day I was born."

I stumbled on a loose rock, almost pulling him over. I

sounded like my mom? Huh. That was new.

Back in the cabin Abby and I examined Uncle Joe's ankle, decided we had no idea what we were looking at, and settled for tucking him into bed while we heated up soup to go with the salad.

"Dude, we are doing good deeds galore," whispered Abby, arranging crackers on a paper plate. "Sprained-ankle rescue? Good deed! Thoughtful salad bringing? Good deed! We'll be in the club in no time."

"We still haven't shown him the salad," I reminded her. "He might just close his eyes and put his fingers in his ears again."

But luckily Uncle Joe didn't start la-la-ing when we shouted "Surprise!" and brought the salad out of the kitchen. He plowed his way through three helpings plus two bowls of soup, and announced that all the fresh greens were making his ankle feel better already. I made up a batch of double-strength cocoa for dessert, Abby cleared away the dishes, and as heavy raindrops started lashing at the windows, Uncle Joe pulled a blanket over himself and fell fast asleep.

With the cabin to ourselves and the whole afternoon stretching ahead, Abby and I resupplied on cocoa, settled in, and got to work brainstorming a backup list of more outstanding good deeds. Just to be prepared. Just in case.

"Will you show me what we've got?" I asked an hour or two later from the arm of the sofa. Abby, sprawled on her back in the entrance to Fort Orpheus, heaved her pad of paper at me. I caught it and read:

Ideas for more good deeds:
- Cook surprise romantic dinner for Dad and Tamal
- Help Joe with his sciency-science research (details to be determined)
- Tune up the twins' bikes for them
- Fill house with flowers as surprise for Maggie's mom
- Find a cat friend for Samson
- Surprise wash Caitlin's ice cream truck
- Other

I smiled to myself. It wasn't much to show for an afternoon's work, but that was fine by me. I hadn't been trying all that hard. The rain was hammering against the windowpanes, the cabin was warm and cozy, and I was just enjoying hanging out with Abby, making plans.

"Okay, so hey," said Abby, running a finger down the list. "These are good, but I see problems with some of them."

"Like what?"

"Like does either of us know how to cook a surprise romantic dinner?"

"Maybe?" I said. I wasn't exactly a top chef, but I was used to eating by myself and could throw together a meal if I had to.

"Well, I definitely can't," said Abby. "And my dad loves cooking, and he's particular about his kitchen. Everything has to be in a certain place or he gets really frustrated. You know how he never lets us put the dishes away when we help wash them? He'd probably be in there with us the whole time, fussing."

"So not really such a good deed, then?"

"Probably not," said Abby. She crossed off the first idea. "Next problem: Can you think of anything we could do, today, that would actually help Joe with his research?"

I thought. We could carry his equipment, maybe, or steer the boat, or organize his recordings, but he could do any of that himself once his foot was better. And if bringing him greens and doing our best to fix his ankle didn't turn out to be enough, I was pretty certain none of that other stuff would be either.

"Um, no."

One by one we crossed off everything on the list, until Uncle Joe woke up with a snort and we had to stop with the fort talk. Pretty soon it was time to say good-bye, and I made Uncle Joe promise to stay off his foot and not go out researching for a while. He agreed, but as Abby and I slipped into the fort, I couldn't shake a nagging prickle of worry about leaving him up there, injured and housebound and alone.

Luckily there were other things to think about as we got back to Seattle.

"Did it work, did it work?" asked Abby. "Did we pass the test?"

"Look for a silver envelope," I said, peering around.

But there was no sign of a silver envelope in Fort McForterson or in Fort Comfy.

"Cucumber casserole!" said Abby. "I was sure that would be enough."

"Sorry," I said. "It was a nice try, though, and at least we made Uncle Joe happy." And me, actually. That was the best afternoon I'd had in a long time.

We ate dinner at Abby's again that night—black bean burgers and coleslaw—and after a push-up contest between Tamal and the twins, and a pileup in the living room for the next superhero movie in the series, Abby and I headed for bed.

I was curled in my usual spot, drowsily dreaming up an arctic-themed sky-versus-ocean game for us to play, when Abby sat bolt upright in the darkness.

"Oh, no!" she said. "We forgot to clean your house!"

I groaned and threw my arms over my face. "Ugh! But we folded the laundry, right? That was the main thing. My mom won't be mad if we do the rest of the house tomorrow."

But Abby was already out of bed and switching on the light. "Dude, no," she said, her hands on her hips. "I want to have tomorrow free for doing good deeds so we can make sure we get into NAFAFA. And that means you need to get up right this second, because tonight we"—she whacked me with her pillow—"are—cleaning!"

It definitely wasn't the best going-over my house had ever seen, but between us we rallied long enough to sweep the floors, polish the faucets, straighten the books, wipe the windows, and scrub the toothpaste out of the bathroom sink before deciding to call it quits.

"Okay, for real, enough's enough," Abby said, as I led the way back into Fort McForterson. "Your mom can't expect us to do more than that."

"I hope no-o-ot," I yawned, closing my eyes as the end of my patchwork scarf brushed over my face. I stopped, wondering sleepily if I could spot the bit of First Sofa in it.

Abby bumped into me headfirst from behind.

"Oop," I said as she fell over, snort-laughing. "Oh, come on, it wasn't that funny." Abby rolled onto her back, sleepy-giggling, and her arm thumped against a pillow one to the right of the entrance.

The pillow fell slowly forward, and another pillow, a *brand-new* pillow, appeared behind it.

THIRTEEN

"Hey!" Abby said. "New link!" And she was right. The off-white, industrial-looking pillow staring back at us was definitely a stranger to Fort McForterson.

"Ugh," I said. "Now? It's seriously too late for this."

"This is awesome!" said Abby, somehow completely awake again. "New link means new fort! But where did it come from?" She pushed the pillow aside. There was darkness behind it. "Only one way to find out!" She started forward.

"Hang on!" I said, throwing out an arm and blocking her path. Questions and dangers were swarming through my tired brain. What if this was a test set by the Council? Or even a trap? Would using this new link disqualify us? Were we supposed to put the pillow back and just forget the link existed? Or were we supposed to explore it and use its powers for good? I couldn't decide.

I couldn't hold Abby back forever either.

"Just, be careful," I said, lowering my arm.

Abby wrinkled her forehead. "Careful? Of what? And why are you always scared of new links?"

"I thought it might be a Council trap. You know, to test us."

"Huh?" said Abby. "How do you figure that? We didn't add this link, so we can't get in trouble for it. It might have nothing to do with them, anyway."

"Then that's even worse," I said. "That means it's a stranger's fort, and that could mean a whole other kind of trouble. I mean"—I waved a hand at the unidentified darkness—"there could be *anything* in there."

Abby rolled her eyes. "Oh, come on, Mags," she said. "This is a *pillow fort*, not a long-lost portal in one of your games. We're not gonna be facing giant spider crabs or hungry ghost badgers. No mechanical librarians are going to kidnap me and hold me for ransom until you hand over a book from your mom's shelves that turns out to be a secret animal-sound translator when you read it in a mirror on the night of a full moon. That's a normal-looking pillow right there, which means it must lead to a normal-enough fort. So why don't we stop wasting time and go check it out?"

Oof. New Abby. She did have some surprisingly good game ideas, though. And it didn't sound like I'd be able to stop her from charging ahead. I sat back and shrugged.

"Thanks," said Abby. "Can you get me some light?"

I passed her a flashlight from my supply corner and watched as she disappeared into the darkness. The seconds ticked by, but nothing happened. No cries for help, no Council bursting in from every pillow, no explosion, no collapsing links. Were we okay, then?

I ran my mind over the Council's lecture about their weird rules, and suddenly remembered the map of Camp Pillow Fort they'd refused to let me see. Our network had made a strange shape on it, bumpier than it looked on our map. Was that because it showed this fort too? A fort that was already linked in, but I just didn't know about it yet? If it had been here all along, it might be okay to use. . . .

A light hit my face from inside the new link. "Hey, Sleepy McTiredface," came Abby's whisper, "come on." I sighed, pushed down my neverending questions, and squeezed in after her.

We were in a small, boxy fort, built around a folding table shoved into a corner. Pillows lined the walls on two sides, with a blanket hanging down to the floor on the others. The cold linoleum floor was littered with art supplies, and as Abby waved her flashlight, I saw colorful drawings taped to the underside of the table above our heads.

"Good thing you were careful coming in," she whispered, "or you might have been seriously injured on all these crayons and pieces of construction paper."

I ignored her.

"It definitely looks like a little kid's fort," Abby went on. "So that's okay. But how did it get linked in? Do you recognize anything?"

I shook my head. Uncle Joe's made sense, but I didn't have the faintest idea how we could've gotten linked in to some random little kid's fort. It felt totally creepy, sneaking around a stranger's space by flashlight. What if the owner turned up and found us? Or worse, what if they were sitting just outside, only inches away on the other side of the blanket, listening to our every word?

And what *was* outside, anyway? Sure, it looked all sweet and innocent in here, but that didn't prove anything. It could all be part of the trap! This fort could be set up in a pitch-black attic, or the musty basement of a haunted mansion, or a locked classroom in an abandoned boarding school, and when we crawled out, we would find our names scrawled on the chalkboard in jagged letters, waiting for us.

"We'll have to go out there and look for clues," I said, shivering.

"Agreed," said Abby. "And it's your turn to go first,

fearless leader." She pointed the flashlight at a crack in the blanket walls. "Watch out for ghost badgers."

"Oh, you are just hilarious tonight," I whispered. Abby giggled.

I took a deep, steadying breath, put my secret-agent shoulders back, parted the sheets the tiniest bit, and looked out.

We were in a hospital room. The walls were pale pastel green, and the cool air smelled like hand sanitizer and paper towels. The lights were turned off, but a computery glow came from a group of machines clustered around a bed on the opposite side of the room.

And in the bed, fast asleep, was a small girl.

"Oh, wow," said Abby, lying flat on her stomach and ducking her head under my arm. I leaned on her shoulders. New Abby sure was a lot more cuddly than Old Abby, and I had to admit, that part was nice. We both watched the girl sleep quietly.

"She must be really sick," I said, scanning the room. "Look at all those cards taped to the wall. She's been here awhile."

There was a soft tap on the door, and it swung open. We scrambled back, killing the flashlight and hardly daring to breathe, as someone came in.

Footsteps crossed the floor toward the bed. There was a

faint click, and one of the machines beeped.

"Mmph, whassat?"

"Hey, Kelly," whispered a voice. "Sorry I woke you. Go back to sleep."

I felt my hair stand on end. I knew that voice. I opened the teeniest crack in the sheet and looked out.

My mom was standing over the bed.

"Deep, slow breaths, sweetie," she said to the girl named Kelly, "and you'll be asleep before you know it. Then when you wake up, it'll be tomorrow and you can play in your pillow fort again."

"Will you be here?"

My mom sat down on the edge of the bed and rested a hand on the little girl's shoulder. "I'll always be right here when you need me," she said.

"Okay," murmured Kelly. "G'night, Dr. Hetzger."

"Good night," whispered my mom. She waited until Kelly was asleep, then adjusted her blankets, scribbled something on a chart at the foot of the bed, and left, closing the door quietly behind her.

I let out a breath.

"Wow," said Abby. "That was weird."

I didn't say a word. It was more than weird. My mom had just promised to be there for this total stranger whenever she needed her. This stranger who wasn't her family, who wasn't her daughter, who wasn't *me*.

Something hot and spiky settled in my stomach.

"That girl's really sick then, isn't she?" said Abby. "Since your mom's a cancer doctor?"

I nodded. We looked out at Kelly. She couldn't have been more than eight.

"And this is her fort," Abby said, shining the flashlight around again. She ran its beam along the pictures taped to the ceiling and smiled. Apparently Kelly liked drawing two things: cats and space. Mostly together. She was good, too. There were cats in space suits, cats on the moon, cats meeting aliens, cats pushing buttons in control rooms, and cats in rockets counting down to liftoff.

The memory of saving Samson from the ice cream truck rocket ship floated through my mind, and I fought back a smile.

"These are adorable," said Abby. "I bet she'd love Samson. And look, crimped edges; she must have scissors like yours, Mags." She nudged me. "You're kindred spirits!"

"Hah," I said.

"I bet she comes in here to pretend she's not in the hospital. It must get really old being sick." Abby flicked a crayon across the floor, then her head snapped up. "Hey! Hey, hey, hey!" She batted me on the shoulder. "We should fix it up for her!"

"What?"

"The fort!" said Abby. "We can give it a makeover, bring her things to make it better, make it fun. It can be a total magical surprise."

"Okay," I said, "but— Ow! Stop it! Why do you always hit people when you have an idea? And please stop calling the forts magical. We're not third graders here."

"What is this thing you have against third graders?" said Abby. "But whatever, this is such a good idea. She'll love it, plus it's the perfect good deed. Win-win!"

I didn't answer. I scowled down at the linoleum.

"Hey," Abby said. "What's up?"

"Nothing," I said. "I just— Don't you think we've done enough good deeds for one night? I'm seriously tired here."

"Come on," said Abby. "It'll be fun. And even forgetting the good deed, this is a nice thing to do. Don't you want to make a sick little kid happy?"

I knew the only answer to that was yes, but I couldn't say it. It wasn't like this Kelly person didn't have time to make her fort better herself. All she had to do was lie around all day while my mom took care of her.

Okay, fine, that wasn't fair. But my stomach still felt hot and spiky, and I definitely wasn't in the mood to stay up late for the second night in a row, doing a favor for someone I didn't even know.

Abby was watching me, a line between her eyebrows

getting deeper and deeper the longer I stayed quiet. I looked away, chewing the inside of my cheek. I wasn't going to win this one.

"Whatever," I said. "Let's get this over with."

"Sweet! Come on, tired Maggie!" Abby shook out her wrists and cracked her neck. "So, what do we need? Or, more important, I guess, what can we get?"

What we got turned out to be a hodgepodge of odds and ends scavenged from our bedrooms and houses. Between us we found: colorful fake flowers to jam between all the pillows; a squashy blue bathmat to spread over the cold floor; a string of paper butterflies; a round mirror with a broken frame; a useful stack of extra construction paper; an old wicker basket to hold Kelly's mess of art supplies; and a miniature tea-party table that we decorated with a lime-green dish towel, a pair of battery-operated candles, a chipped teacup, and a tiny owl wearing a hat.

It was hard work crawling back and forth with our hands full, especially since we were trying to be quiet, and by the time we finished even Abby was grumbling. Still, as we sat back to survey the final result, I couldn't help feeling a rush of pride at what we'd done. We'd transformed Kelly's boring, everyday fort into a cozy palace, pretty and twinkling in the electric candlelight.

"Go us!" said Abby, wiping her forehead. "This is awesome. Kelly's going to be over the moon."

"Along with her cats," I said, nodding up at the drawings.

"Ha!" said Abby. "There's my girl back."

I flashed her a grin, then dropped it as a new worry suddenly occurred to me. What if Kelly wasn't over the moon? What if she got scared instead? What if we came back to visit and found her fort surrounded by police tape, with all those knickknacks covered in our fingerprints sealed up in plastic bags as evidence? If Kelly took the makeover the wrong way, we could be in serious, serious trouble.

"Calm down," said Abby when I pointed out the problem. "It's okay. We can leave her a note. That way she'll know someone nice was behind everything."

After carefully discussing how much to say, we wrote out the note.

Dear Kelly,

Surprise! We hope you like your fort makeover. We can't tell you who we are, but we have forts too, so we're kindred spirits.

Your space cat pictures are awesome! Will you draw us one of a big black-and-white cat? We know a cat like that. His name is Samson. He hasn't been to outer space, but he likes to explore and go back and forth between our forts. We are so sorry you have to be in the hospital and hope you get well very, very soon.

From . . .

"What should we put?" asked Abby, tapping the pen on her leg. "'A & M'?"

"'Your Forty Godmothers'?" I suggested.

"How about 'Your Next-Fort Neighbors'?" said Abby.

"That works."

Abby folded up the letter and tucked it under a candle on the little table.

"Okay, that's that," she said, rubbing her eyes. "Guess all we can do now is wait to see if she likes it. But hey"—she bopped me on the knee—"at least now we can be absolutely, for sure certain we're in NAFAFA. If thoughtful greens, ankle fixing, housecleaning, and heroic fort fancying don't get us in, nothing will."

She yawned. Then I yawned. Then both of us yawned, and we made our last trip home for the night.

Abby went back to her place, but I decided I needed a change after the long day and crawled up onto my old sofa bunk in Fort McForterson. It was glorious getting to stretch out in my own space again, and I realized being on my own didn't bother me at all now that my best friend was right on the other side of the pillow.

Besides, I thought as I finally drifted off to sleep, *Abby was right: there was no way we weren't in NAFAFA now. All the hard work was behind us, and from here on out, things could only get easier.*

FOURTEEN

I woke the next morning to the blare of my house phone ringing in the kitchen. I crawled out of the fort and shuffled over to answer it.

"Hullo?" I said, staring blearily at the stove clock. It read 8:05 a.m.

"Maggles, it's Abby."

My brain gave a hiccup. That didn't compute. Why would Abby call me on the house phone? It would have been faster to just reach through the forts and poke me.

"Who?"

"Abby, your best friend and next-door neighbor. Listen, we've got trouble."

My brain hiccupped again, slowly coming online.

"Huh? What sort of trouble?"

"Well, for starters, I'm grounded."

My brain thudded into gear.

"Grounded? What for?"

"My dad woke me up a bit ago kind of . . . very angry," she said. There was a quaver in her voice. It took a lot to upset Abby. "He asked me to come look at something in the kitchen, and it was a total mess. Everything in the cupboards was switched around, and the mugs were under the stove, and the pots and pans were in the freezer, and there were dirty fingerprints on the walls, and all the forks and knives were hidden in the orange juice carton. It was chaos."

"What?!"

"And Mags, he thinks we did it. He said he heard us sneaking around last night and just assumed we were playing a game, but if this is our idea of a practical joke, it's going too far. I told him it wasn't us, but he asked me who it was then and I couldn't think of anything to say, and so now I'm grounded." She let out a shaky breath. "It was NAFAFA, wasn't it, Mags? They attacked."

I nodded, forgetting she couldn't see me. "It must have been—there's no other explanation. But *why*?"

"I don't know. This is all just really messed up. Is everything okay at your place?"

I looked around the kitchen and what I could see of the living room. Everything looked normal, except, wait—we'd totally straightened all those lopsided books, and where did that dirt on the floor come from? And the smears on the windows? You'd never know Abby and I had cleaned at all. I caught sight of a folded piece of paper propped on the stove, my name on the front in all caps. My stomach dropped.

"Um, maybe not. Can you hang on a second?"

I opened the note and skimmed it, my stomach sinking further and further with every line.

"Okay, more bad news," I said, getting back on the phone. "I'm grounded too. My mom left a note saying the house was a wreck when she got home late last night. She says it looked like we did our best to *un-clean* everything, and if we think tying all the laundry in knots and shoving it under her bed was a funny joke, then we have some serious growing up to do."

"They undid all our cleaning? And the laundry folding?" said Abby. "That's horrible. And—dude, that means they were listening when we brainstormed up in Alaska! Remember I said my dad was picky about his kitchen? That must be where they got the idea. They did all this on purpose just to get us in trouble!"

"And it worked," I said grimly. "My mom says she cleaned up most of the mess before going back to the hospital, but we're going to have a very serious talk as soon as she gets home."

"Oh, I'm so sorry, Mags."

"I'll survive. My mom never has time to give really bad lectures."

"Well, I feel completely awful," said Abby. "I can't stand my dad being mad at me! How are we going to fix this?"

"We need to come up with a plan. Say you're going to your room and meet me in my fort."

I hung up the phone and read through my mom's note again. It was a NAFAFA attack for sure, but why? Why undo all our hard work, and frame us for it too, when we'd just spent an entire day doing good deeds?

I flipped over the note and found a PS on the back.

By the way, I found the good flashlight in your pillow fort. Please stop taking things from around the house and hiding them in there. The other day I spent twenty minutes trying to find a pair of scissors that should have been in the kitchen, and by the time I found them behind your postcard box, I was almost late for work. Try to be a good housemate and show a little more respect for my belongings.

Oof. By my mom's standards that was practically yelling. But there was something else in there, something that nagged at me, apart from my mom. I read through the PS again. It seemed normal enough, but I couldn't shake the feeling I was missing something important.

There was another surprise waiting for me when I reached Fort McForterson: a shiny silver envelope with my name on the front. Abby linked over just as I was opening it. She looked miserable.

"Hey!" she said. "Is that from the Council?"

I nodded. "They must have left it while we were on the phone."

"Let me see." We put our heads together and read.

To: Maggie Hetzger, Vice Director, Camp Pillow Fort
From: The Council of NAFAFA

This is your official notification of censure from the Council of NAFAFA. As an applicant for membership in our organization, you were provided with certain regulations and guidelines to follow. Below is a list of the rules, regulations, and guidelines you have been found to have violated.

1) Adding new forts to your network.
(Location: Greenway Children's Hospital. Builder Name: Kelly. Age: 8. Approved: NO.)
(Addendum: Certain Council members want to clarify that the Council is aware the link to Kelly's was created

accidentally and is therefore not technically a violation. Others, however, believe that upon discovering a new link while under consideration for membership, you should have voluntarily ignored it until membership was granted, thereby respecting the spirit of the law as well as the letter.)

2) Telling anyone not already involved about fort network/s. (Location: Greenway Children's Hospital. Name: Kelly. Age: 8. Approved: NO.)

(Addendum: Council not unanimous on this point either. Some of us believe performing an otherwise inexplicable makeover on a fort is the same as telling about the network; others do not. The letter written by Abby Hernandez added weight to the argument for censure, dealing as it did with fort access and manipulation, and in the end we decided to note the violation. While Kelly may not know the hows and whys of what has happened to her fort, she is sure to understand that something out of the ordinary is going on with it, something she would not have been aware of without your actions or your letter.)

Due to these somewhat unclear violations, an appropriately calibrated reprimand has been carried out. You have been warned. Another violation of our regulations and guidelines will result in a full-scale attack.

You are now officially on probation. Remember there are just under two days remaining for you to fulfill your obligations and perform a good deed up to NAFAFA standards, or your application for membership will be rejected and your network permanently terminated.

Have a nice day.

Sincerely,

The Council of NAFAFA

"I bet you anything Ben wrote that," I said, glaring at the note.

"Dude," said Abby. "That is some serious cucumber casserole right there! I did not tell Kelly too much in the note. I barely told her anything. And what do they mean about her link being 'accidentally created'?"

"I have a guess about that." My brain had finally put two and two together, and I was pretty sure I was right. "Remember how you said Kelly and I were kindred spirits because we both owned crimping scissors?"

"Yeah..."

"I think it was actually the same pair."

"Huh? Explain, please."

I showed her the PS in my mom's note. "I think she meant her crimping scissors," I said, "and I think she took them to

* 171 *

work and gave them to Kelly for her arts and crafts."

"So your mom was the one who added the new fort," said Abby slowly. "And we're the ones who got in trouble for it?"

"Kind of makes you want to scream, doesn't it?" I said.

"Of course it does!" said Abby. "We did tons of good deeds yesterday, *and* we made a sick kid really happy, and those Council kids still attacked us. I've never been in trouble like this before! How am I going to—"

But she was interrupted as one of the wall pillows came flying into the fort and a kid in silver sunglasses appeared in its place.

I felt my mouth fall open.

It was Noriko.

FIFTEEN

"Hey! What—?" I said, just as Abby said, "Dude! Who—?"

Noriko gave us a short nod.

"Hello again, Maggie Hetzger," she said. "And hello, Abby Hernandez. My name is Noriko. I'm Head of the Council of NAFAFA and Chancellor of the Forts of the Eastern Seaboard."

Abby gaped at her. "You're one of the ones who sent the letter."

Noriko nodded again, making her earrings—dangly silver penguins this time—dance in the lamplight. There was a pause, and then Abby and I both started shouting at once.

"—totally outrageous—"

"—poor little kid—"

"—and your sunglasses, too!"

"I am here," said Noriko, raising a hand and speaking over us, "to make sure you received your letter of reprimand and understand the contents."

We were both telling her exactly what we thought of her letter of reprimand when Noriko put a finger to her lips in a *shh* signal, pulled a slip of paper from her pocket, and held it out. Abby and I stopped shouting, our voices trailing off. I took the paper.

"I know our policies at NAFAFA can be very hard for novices such as yourselves to understand," Noriko said as though nothing had happened, "and as head of the Council it's my duty to make sure we're communicating with you effectively. An uncertain network does no one any favors."

She nodded meaningfully at the paper. I unfolded it, and Abby crowded around to read.

Hi! Ask me to show you the collecting room Murray told you about. ACT NATURAL.

We looked up at her.

"So, do you have any questions you'd like to ask?" Noriko said deliberately.

I blinked. Abby nudged me.

"Oh. Um, okay, yes." I glanced back at the note. "I was wondering if you would show us that collecting room Murray told me about. The one where all the coins go. Or that's what he told me. When Murray told me about the room. Anyway, could we see it?"

I hoped that counted as acting natural. Noriko smiled and gave a thumbs-up.

"What a strange request," she said loudly. "But I suppose it would be all right. Follow me." She backed out of the link, and Abby and I crawled after her into the Hub.

Abby didn't have to try acting natural when she stood up and looked around. Her reaction was perfect. She gaped at the mammoth patchwork ceiling, the maze of sofas and shelves, the curving pillow wall, and the gleaming chandelier.

Noriko led the way along the wall to the left, and I followed behind, trying not to show how much I was enjoying watching Abby gawk and stare.

It was busier in the Hub than it had been during my midnight visit. The place was packed. A group of girls ran through the crowd just ahead of us, playing what looked like some kind of badminton tag. One aisle over, a circle of older-looking kids holding scripts was acting out a play, complete with dramatic crying and bad British accents. A paper airplane arced over a cluster of forts made of beach umbrellas and neon-pink towels, and a hand reached out of the forts and caught it. A moment later there was a shout of laughter, and a plastic soda bottle with a roll of paper inside went flying back the other way, just missing a line of boys in hockey jerseys fencing with foam pool noodles.

Abby fell back and grabbed my arm. "Mags, this is the best thing I've ever seen in my whole life! Look at all these kids we get to meet!"

Suddenly the badminton birdie whizzed by out of nowhere, landing with a plonk a few feet from us, and the girls with rackets burst out of the fort maze in hot pursuit. Abby got there first, scooped it up, and ran down to hand it over. I watched, impressed at her courage. These girls were total strangers! One of them said something as she took back the birdie, then Abby said something, raising both hands, and next second the whole group was laughing. A tall girl with braces held out her racket and pointed to the maze, clearly inviting Abby to join them, and I went from being impressed to being flat-out astonished. Seriously, how did Abby do that?

Abby shook her head, smiling, and trotted back to me. "This place is so great!" she said, turning and waving at the badminton girls. They waved back. I hesitated, then gathered my courage and waved too, but they were disappearing into the maze and didn't see. I looked around to find Abby and Noriko already several pillows away. I had to jog to catch up.

At last we reached the enormous pillow with the metallic clinking sounds behind it, and Noriko stopped and faced us. Just down the wall a round pillow covered in clear plastic swung open, and a boy wearing swimming goggles and a tank top stepped into the Hub. He was covered from the waist down in thick soap bubbles. Abby giggled.

"Hey, ma'am," the boy called, waving at Noriko.

"Hi, Connor," she said. "How was the match? Are you still undefeated?" Connor grinned and gave a double thumbs-up, then strutted out onto the main floor, where he was immediately hit by a badminton birdie.

"Okay," Noriko said, turning to us again. "Business, Maggie Hetzger. What did Murray tell you about this room?" She put a hand on the massive pillow door.

I pulled my question-packed brain back to what we were doing. The Hub was very distracting. "He told me this is where you collect all the coins that fall down the back of sofas," I said.

"Basically correct," said Noriko. "Which means the room is a little noisy. Get ready."

She gave a push and the pillow swung open, releasing a solid wall of sound. We followed her inside.

It was like stepping into the engine room of one of Kelly's spaceships. A forest of gleaming metal tubes stretched far overhead and descended in a tangle through a metal-grating floor at our feet. The noise coming from them was incredible: an echoing roar of clinking, clanking, plinking, banging, and clanging.

Noriko led the way through the maze of twisting pipes to a wide hole in the floor with a railing around it. Below us the tubes were spilling out a steady stream of shining coins into huge vats. We all put our elbows on the railing and leaned over to look.

"So," said Noriko, shouting over the noise. "I've asked you here today because this is the only place I can speak freely without potentially being overheard."

Abby and I exchanged a look.

"This isn't just about coin collecting, then?" I asked.

"No. That part's pretty obvious, I think." She gestured to the vats below. "This is a much bigger issue."

"Ooh," said Abby. "Intrigue!"

"First of all," said Noriko, "I want to apologize for the attack. I didn't want it to happen. I thought what you did for Kelly should have counted as a good deed; but others on the Council didn't and they forced my hand and I'm sorry. I kept the attack as mild as I could, though."

"Mild?" Abby said, her smile dropping. "You call that mild? My dad said he never thought he'd be this disappointed in me in his entire life!"

"You seriously damaged our relationship with our parents," I said.

"Well, yeah," said Noriko. "That is the point of our attacks, Maggie. I told you that going in. Anyway, I did my best to minimize it and now I've apologized, so let's move on." She straightened up. "Okay, so the super exciting secret you two don't know yet is that you're actually caught up in the middle of the biggest power struggle NAFAFA has ever had. Things are changing fast around here, and with your help I can make sure everything turns out the way it should."

"A power struggle over what?" asked Abby.

"Territory," said Noriko. "And this is important, so pay attention, please. Right now, the four major NAFAFA networks each control a different section of North America. The easy way to explain is to say I control the right-hand side of the continent, Murray controls the top, Miesha controls the bottom, and Ben controls the middle. You might want to close your eyes and picture that."

"Oh, no," I said, shaking my head. "No way am I getting Lisa Franked again!"

"Ooo, good save!" said Abby, nudging me with her elbow.

Noriko snorted. "Oh, come on, that's Miesha's trick, not mine. I promise I'm not going to start talking about teal zebras and magenta glitter kittens. You can keep your eyes open, just picture the continent like I said. Notice anything unaccounted for?"

I spread out a map in my brain, plugging in the Council members where Noriko had said, then nodded. "The left side."

"Exactly. And that's because for the entire history of NAFAFA there's never been a functioning network on the west coast. Until yours."

Abby straightened up too. "Wait, for real?" she said. "How is that possible?"

"No one's sure," said Noriko. "We keep an eye out, obviously, but we've always just assumed scraps of the First Sofa never made it that far. You two total novices are officially the first, and according to the NAFAFA charter that means once you're accepted, you automatically get a seat on the Council and every pillow fort built along the west coast of North America from now on will be under your control. That, Maggie Hetzger, is why your group is a special case. Congratulations."

Abby raised both hands above her head. "Whoo!" she said. "Go, Camp Pillow Fort!"

"Huh," I said. "Wow."

"And after we join, can we add new forts?" Abby asked, her eyes wide. "As many new forts as we want?"

Noriko nodded. "After a few weeks of training and orientation, yeah, as many as you want."

"Sweet!" Abby whapped me on the arm. "Mags, it's perfect! I can send tokens to all my friends from camp, and this time next week we'll have new members all over the state! Plus one of my friends has family in California, and I bet you anything someone knows some kids up in Vancouver. We can build our own version of Camp Cantaloupe in no time!"

Her face was shining with happiness, but I felt like I'd tumbled over the railing and fallen headfirst into one of the vats. Making friends with the badminton girls in the Hub was one thing, but now Abby was talking about opening up our network to every random kid from Camp Cantaloupe? What was wrong with the way things had been? What was wrong with just the two of us?

I swallowed hard. It was finally starting to sink in that what Abby really wanted out of this whole adventure was more time with other people. Other people who weren't me.

"Hold on," I said, shoving down my feelings. I could be sad later. Right now there were critical secret-agent issues to address, like Noriko's offer sounding way too good to possibly be true. "You're saying you and the rest of the Council are just going to hand us all this territory and power? What's the catch?"

"There's no catch," said Noriko. "But there is one short, annoying obstacle. And he has a seat on the Council."

"Ben?" I said.

"Ben."

"Is that Overall Boy?" asked Abby.

Noriko laughed. "Ha! That's what Connor calls him. Yeah, Ben's being kind of a roadblock. He wants the west coast for himself, and he's trying to get you disqualified before you can even complete your task. He's the one who pointed out all the technical violations last night that led to the attack, and the one who wrote the letter."

"Called it," I said.

"But how could he ever get the west coast?" Abby asked. "Isn't he in charge of the Midwest Sofa Oval, or whatever?"

"The Great Plains Sofa Circle," said Noriko. "Yeah, he is. But NAFAFA's been divided over what to do with the west for decades. I mean, it's just been sitting there, cut off, as far as forts are concerned. Do you know how weird it is to be linked up with kids from all over the entire continent but not have a single pillow fort from California? It's pretty weird.

"My network and Murray's have always voted to leave the west alone, because honestly we have enough territory to deal with already. Miesha's network wanted it for a while back in the late 1900s but they don't anymore. But Ben's network has wanted to stretch out to the west coast this whole entire time, and Ben thinks they've waited long enough. Getting it would make Ben's network bigger and more powerful than any of the others, and I can't let that happen. Partly because, you know, it's *Ben*. But mostly because my network has always been the biggest, and the most fun, and I refuse to be the head of the Council who lets that change."

Oof. So much drama and intrigue going on under all these

pillows and banners! Didn't these kids know they could have an adventure without it turning into a soap opera? "So stop him," I said. "You're in charge, aren't you?"

"I have stopped him," said Noriko. "I've blocked Ben over and over, but I turn thirteen next month, I'm aging out, and he's been waiting for that exact chance since the minute he joined.

"Except now we've got you two, in the nick of time, and if we can get you through your good-deed test and onto the Council before I leave, then all his plans will be shot and my legacy and NAFAFA will be safe."

Abby raised her hand, frowning. "Okay, so I get that Ben wants the west and you won't let him have it," she said. "But how does you aging out give him his chance? Can't the next leader just keep blocking him?"

Noriko shook her head. "That's the main problem right there. The charter says it takes four votes to elect someone to run the Council. Obviously, I want Miesha to get it, and she's the next oldest, but Ben's made it clear the only way he'll vote for anyone but himself is if we agree to let him take over the west coast first. Before we elect a new head. But if we can get your network onto the Council, we'll have the four votes we need for Miesha, and there's nothing he can do to stop it."

"Bad luck for Ben," said Abby cheerfully.

"Totally," said Noriko. "He actually thinks this is all super suspicious. He thinks I set up your network on purpose in order to block him at the last minute. That's why we're sneaking around like this. He's got his spies everywhere. Miesha's on 'Distract Ben' duty with Sprinkles the puppy right now just so we could have this meeting."

"Aww!" said Abby. "Puppy duty!"

"Is that why Ben was being so unfriendly when I met him the other day?" I asked.

"Yup," said Noriko. "I mean, Ben's never exactly been sweet, but he knows you two turning up could stop his dreams of expansion for good, *and* he thinks I'm helping you. That's making him an extra-grumpy Overall Boy." She leaned against the railing, crossing her arms. "So, yeah, that's the situation. This *has* to happen, and I'm sorry to be blunt, but it's pretty clear from all your flailing around that you two can't do this on your own. That's why I've organized everything for you and set up a foolproof, can't-fail good deed. It's a sure thing, and totally doable even though you're grounded. Carolina is putting the finishing touches in place and dropping off instructions in your fort right now."

The roar of the room thundered around us.

"But that's . . . cheating, isn't it?" I said, blinking. "Isn't that exactly what Ben's accusing you of? That's got to be against the rules."

"Maybe? Technically? Who knows?" said Noriko. "Please don't go quoting regulations at me, Maggie Hetzger. I'm head of the Council, and I can tell you half our rules are ridiculous anyway. Take the silver sunglasses." She tapped her frames. "They're just ordinary sunglasses. We started wearing them when the Hub chandelier got brighter bulbs back in the seventies. It started as a joke, but some Ben-type kid decided they should be a sign of authority and somehow made it against regulations to even talk about them, like you found out when you asked. Half our rules are completely pointless and entirely weird, and I think that means we can bend them sometimes if we have to. It's not like we're keeping Ben from getting anything he should actually have, anyway. We're just maintaining the balance."

Abby caught my eye, her fingers playing with the end of her braid. She arched an eyebrow. I wasn't certain what that meant, so I raised mine back.

Noriko was watching us. "Look," she said, an edge of exasperation in her voice, "I don't think this is that hard. This is the part where you decide what you want. Do you want to take the next step and join the big leagues of pillow forts? Or do you want to go back to playing those make-believe games you keep talking about? It seems like an easy choice to me, but maybe I've been wrong about you.

"I can guarantee your acceptance into NAFAFA if you just jump through the hoops and avoid breaking the rules for anything less than a genuine, life-or-death emergency for the next couple of days. And remember, if you don't pass the test, we're shutting you down anyway. You'll never do a good enough deed on your own in that time, so this really is your only chance. I'm trying to make it easy on you here."

The jangling pipes and coins seemed to grow louder as Noriko finished her speech.

I didn't know what to say. My insides were feeling as tangled as the room around us. Everything had changed. First Abby wanted to turn the whole west coast into one giant summer camp reunion, then Noriko admitted she'd been openly using us, moving us around like pawns in her power games. She had kind of threatened us too. Didn't her whole argument boil down to *Do what I say or else*?

And hey, who was she to say we were *flailing* and couldn't come up with a top-notch good deed in time? We'd just done three in one day! We didn't need her shortcuts. We could do it ourselves.

And if for some weird reason it didn't work out, well, then fine, we'd lose the links. But I'd still have Abby, and we'd still have our games. And no matter what Noriko said, that sounded just fine to me. It would sting losing Alaska, but this was about principles now. We'd make it into NAFAFA on our own or not have a network at all.

I looked over at Abby, who smiled and gave me a single, determined nod. This time I understood perfectly. We didn't even have to speak. *We are Camp Pillow Fort,* that smile and nod were saying, *and we can meet this challenge together, just the two of us.* I grinned and nodded back.

"We'll have to think about it," I said to Noriko. There was no point giving her a direct answer just yet. We had plans to make first. Glorious plans.

"Of course," said Noriko. "I expected that. I've arranged for Carolina to be your audio surveillance officer this afternoon. You'll have a two-hour window once you're back where you can talk freely."

"Great," I said. "Thanks."

Noriko narrowed her eyes at me, then sighed. "Okay, look, to show you how serious I am, I'll throw in a bonus: follow my instructions, do this right, and I'll do everything in my power to fix your relationships with your parents. I'll personally make sure they know you weren't responsible, and everything will be like it was before."

"You can do that?" asked Abby, her eyes wide.

"I'm Head of the Council of NAFAFA and Chancellor of the Forts of the Eastern Seaboard," said Noriko. "Of course I can."

"Wow!" said Abby. "Also, hey, can I ask a totally off-topic question?"

Noriko shrugged.

"What's in that big tank in the corner?"

We all looked down. The big tank in the corner was full of something, but it wasn't coins. It looked more like . . .

"Cheerios," said Noriko. "You wouldn't believe how many Cheerios end up falling down the back of sofas. We had to put them somewhere."

Abby whistled, impressed. She gazed around at the forest of pipes. "So, how does all this work?"

"Do your good deed, get into NAFAFA, and you'll find out," Noriko said. "But I'm tired of shouting here. You know where I stand. I'll take you back to your own network, and then you two have a big decision to make."

SIXTEEN

"Leave it to us to wander into a pillow fort civil war," I said as the link closed behind us.

"I know," Abby said, "it's bizarre. But that Hub! It's incredible! You really didn't describe it well enough. And all those other kids we can hang out with! I can't wait to get into NAFAFA now."

She seized the silver envelope waiting in the middle of the floor and ripped it open. "Let's see what this maybe technically cheating good deed is." She cleared her throat and read the letter aloud.

Maggie Hetzger & Abby Hernandez,
    Your good deed has been prepared. Please follow these instructions carefully. The blue-striped pillow two to the

left of the entrance of your hub has been linked to what we call a 'partial fort.' That means a situation where the pieces needed for a linked fort (pillows, a basic covering, a token) are gathered by accident. This mostly happens on sofas, like the one you encountered when you first linked up to Alaska. The partial we've set up for you today is a tarp and sofa in an alley behind the garbage dump half a mile from your house, and since it's not a formal pillow fort, linking there is totally fine within the NAFAFA rules and regulations, even for a network on probation, and even with Ben nosing around.

The alley is a mess. The maintenance man who usually takes care of anything dumped there is getting old, and the trash has been piling up. You will clean the alley for him. Link through, clean the alley, talk about doing it later tonight when a regular monitor is on duty, and I'll take the report and spin it up to good-deed status.

It's important that you do a very thorough job, since the Council will judge you on the end result. It'll probably take you a combined four to six hours of hard work. Sorry about that, but we need it to look convincing.

Maggie, Murray says you like spotting problems and asking lots of questions, so you're probably wondering how we've linked the alley to your fort and what the cover story is. The 'how' is we took a postcard from your shoe box and tucked it under the sofa cushions. The cover story is you threw the card away and it got blown out of the recycling truck and ended up in the alley. Talking about that in your fort once the regular monitor is back on duty would be helpful. You could even say that maybe a rat found the postcard and carried it into the sofa to make a nest.

I don't think there are any rats in the alley, but there might be. Sorry about that, too.

Sincerely,

Noriko, Head of the Council of NAFAFA, Chancellor of the Forts of the Eastern Seaboard

"Really?" I said, staring down at the letter. "More cleaning? Good thing that's not happening!"

"What?" said Abby. "I think it sounds fine. We can get a start now, come back home for lunch, then finish up tonight. We get accepted tomorrow, Noriko fixes things with our families, and *bam*, all our problems are solved! She made it pretty convenient."

"Wait, wait, wait. Hang on," I said. "Are you saying you want to do this?"

"Obviously," said Abby. "Wait. Are you saying you don't?"

"Of course!"

Abby frowned. "Um, okay. Why not?"

Why were we even having this conversation? I held up

three fingers. "I don't want to clean up an old, dirty alley; I don't want to get into NAFAFA using someone else's 'maybe technically cheating' plan; and I don't want to do what Noriko says just because she tells us to."

"Oh. Huh," said Abby. She held up three fingers of her own. "Well, I want Noriko to fix things with my dad; I don't mind hard work when it's helping someone; and I don't want to miss out and spend the rest of the summer wondering about all the adventures we could be having if we just went with the flow and got into this NAFAFA club when we had the chance. Besides, Noriko's only doing what's best for her network, Mags. There's no reason to take any of this personally."

I felt like my brain had missed a step. "But—but what about back in the collecting room? That nod, when we agreed not to do this because we could do it ourselves?"

"What are you talking about?" said Abby. "I was nodding yes, all right, let's do this. I was agreeing with Noriko."

My insides flipped over. Once again, New Abby had come along and yanked the rug right out from under me.

"Huh, okay," I said. Time for a deep, slow breath. "But don't you think it would be better if we brainstormed more good deeds and passed the NAFAFA test on our own? We can do it—we're Camp Pillow Fort!"

"There's not enough time, Mags," Abby said, shaking her

head. "Like Noriko told us, this is our only option."

"No, it's not."

"Yeah, it is."

"Not."

"Is!"

"Not!"

We glared at each other.

"Just so I know, are you speaking in code right now?" I asked.

"No. And why do you keep thinking that?"

"Because you sound different." I heard a tremor in my voice. "Something happened to you this summer."

"Yeah," declared Abby. "It did. I had a great time at Camp Cantaloupe. And I want to keep that going now that I'm home. And that means getting into NAFAFA, and this is how we're doing it. Look"—she crossed her arms—"do you have even one new good-deed idea? One that's ready to go right now?"

I had to shake my head.

"See? Sorry if it bugs you, Mags, but we're cleaning up the alley, and that's final."

"No, we're not," I said, indignation flaring up inside me. First Noriko, now my own best friend telling me what to do? No way. "I'm head of our network, and I say we're not doing it."

"Oh, so I automatically have to follow your orders?" Abby

fired back. "Uh-uh. My cat's technically in charge, in case you forgot. And you may be vice director, but you don't order me around."

I spluttered. "What?! You're ordering me around!"

"No, you are!" said Abby. "You're saying I have to do what you say or you won't play with me!"

My stomach twisted painfully. This was all going wrong. "I'm not saying that," I said slowly. "All I'm saying is I want us to come up with our own plan instead of taking Noriko's. Like we always used to."

"Fine, then I'll do Noriko's good deed without you," said Abby, shrugging.

"You can't," I insisted. "You can't just decide to split up the group and go with her plan over mine."

"Mags, you just said you don't have a plan," said Abby. "And stop trying to make me your sidekick in all this. Believe it or not, I can have adventures on my own!"

"So, what? You're just going to go off and leave me behind like before?" The words were out of my mouth before I could stop them.

There was a thunderously uncomfortable silence.

Abby put a hand over her mouth. "Oh, dude. Is that what this is about? Are you still mad about me going away to camp?"

"No!"

"Really sounds like it."

"Does not."

"Yeah, it does."

I took a super deep breath and held it, feeling the blood pounding behind my ears. "I'm not mad you went," I said, letting it all out at once and fighting hard to keep my voice steady. "I just . . . missed you."

"Well, I'm sorry about that," said Abby. "But it's not enough reason for me to feel bad about deciding to go."

I blinked away the rainbows in the corners of my eyes. "What? You told me you didn't have a choice. You said your dad made you go since he couldn't get a refund."

"Oh, yeah . . ." Abby went very still. Her face flushed dark. "Um, about that." Her eyes flicked to mine, then away again. "So, actually . . . I went on purpose. We could have gotten a refund. I could have stayed home. But when my dad asked me if we should cancel after you missed the deadline, I thought about it and decided I really, really wanted to go, even if you couldn't."

My heart stopped dead. The pillows spun around me. For one horrible moment I honestly thought I was falling through the carpet. I asked the only question I could think of.

"Why?"

"Because I didn't want to miss out," said Abby. There was a plea in her voice. "I needed something different this summer, Mags, I just did. I needed—I needed to start actually *doing* things and not just hang out with you imagining all the time. Your games are great, don't get me wrong, but they're not really my thing anymore, and with middle school coming up . . . Only I never really figured out a way to tell you, and then camp was starting . . ." She took a deep breath. "Look, I'm sorry if you were sad. Truly. Ever since I got back I've been trying to share as much of camp as I could with you, and I do honestly wish you'd been there, but it's done now. It's over. And I'm not sorry I went."

It sounded like a practiced speech.

"But why didn't you tell me?" I said around the lump in my throat. "Did you think I wouldn't understand or something?"

"Honestly . . . ?" said Abby. She left the answer hanging, hovering in the air between us. "Look, I know you're mad, but I said I was sorry and we can't change it now, so let's just move on." She tugged at her braid, and a crease appeared between her eyebrows. "And you can ease up on whatever abandoned-castaway story you're probably starting in your head. It's not like I'm gonna make this a habit or anything."

The unfairness of that statement shocked me. "But you're already doing the exact same thing!" I said, jabbing a finger at the silver envelope. "You're choosing to leave me behind again right now."

"No," said Abby, firing up. "I'm choosing to follow through on something I think is important, and you're choosing not to come! This is exactly why I didn't tell you before, Mags, because you always take everything personally. Not everything I do is about you!"

She exhaled hard and sat back, slumping against the sofa with her arms crossed.

I couldn't speak. I was having trouble breathing. I stared down at one of the pillowcases, my vision going blurry.

"Anyway," I finally heard her say, "we're wasting time. I'm going to the alley. I'm taking Noriko's offer, and I could really use your help."

I shook my head. I was not going to cry.

"Hey," she said, scooching closer and bopping me on the knee. "Remember how freaked out you were about the link that led to Joe's at first? And the one to Kelly's? I had to push you there, and it all turned out fine. This is like that. It might sound scary or strange at first, but this is how we're gonna make everything okay. Me and you. By our powers combined. Together."

Every knot in my stomach clenched. She was trying to get me to rally, but she was only making it worse.

She was really saying she hadn't needed me all those other times, and she hadn't needed me when she went away to camp, and she didn't need me now.

And maybe I didn't need her, either.

I shook my head.

Abby watched me for a long moment, then reached out and pulled away the blue-striped pillow, revealing a torn and grimy sofa cushion leaning at an angle. Without a word, without even glancing back, she disappeared through the link and shoved it closed behind her.

SEVENTEEN

There's no sound in the world quite like the sound of your best friend walking out on you.

I'd imagined plenty of awful things in my eleven and a half years of life. Epic disasters, terrible accidents, collisions, storms, floods, and invasions. And I'd always known how to deal with them. I'd always planned, and prepared, and found a way to make them right. But never once in my entire life had I imagined Abby might leave me.

I had no plan for this.

Still, there I was, all alone again in my silent, overgrown, rat-people nest, the fight with Abby bouncing off the pillows and echoing around my brain.

I sat up to leave, steadying myself against the pillow Abby had been leaning on. It was still warm. I suddenly remembered how she hugged me the day she came home from camp, and my heart seized up.

I fled to the kitchen.

The clock ticked as I walked from one side of the floor to the other, smacking at the counters. I yanked open the fridge, making the juice carton and yogurts wobble. There was plenty of good food in there. Abby and I had cleaned out most of the vegetables making the salad for Uncle Joe, but—

I slammed the fridge shut. I didn't want to think about food if that meant thinking about Abby. I glared around. There was the house phone. What if I called my mom at work? Maybe she could distract me. Except, no, I was grounded and in trouble, and that's what she would want to talk about. Not that I could really tell her why my heart was in tatters.

I abandoned the kitchen and went up on the roof.

It was hot. The sun was beating down hard on the shingles. I wrapped my arms around my knees, tightened my jaw, took a deep, slow breath, and made a firm decision to stop feeling sad. Choices had been made, lines had been drawn, and there was no point wasting time thinking about it. I was going to sit there, rally, and be fine.

I tried thinking about nice things like Matt's arms, Samson's purr, and peach ice cream, then realized I was staring straight at the same pine tree I'd stared at every day when I was waiting for Abby to come home.

"Ugh!" I said to the tree, the roof, and the whole tangled,

broken summer in general. Abby was everywhere around here, and the bright sun was making my eyes water. I needed the opposite of all this.

I climbed off the roof and tromped to Alaska.

* * *

There was a note on the floor outside Fort Orpheus. It was addressed to me. I opened it, wondering exactly when my life had become a nonstop parade of cards and notes and letters.

> Dear Maggie,
>
> If you're reading this, it means you're in my cabin and I'm not, which probably means you're mad at me. I know I promised to stay off my foot, but my ankle felt 99% back to normal this morning, and I just couldn't miss doing my field recordings two days in a row. Sorry!
>
> Love, Uncle Joe

I rolled my eyes and went to the window. The sky was as heavy and gray as a humpback's belly again, and there was Uncle Joe, stretched out on his back beside his boat with his listening equipment set up around him.

Well, at least he hadn't tried to go out on the water. I decided to let him get on with it. I was feeling way too jangly to be good company right then, anyway.

Not that I was being very good company for myself. I

was totally restless. I stalked around the cabin, opening cupboards, kicking random bits of furniture, and fiddling with the equipment piled on the desk. A switch hooked up to an old speaker was too tempting not to flick, and as it clicked on a strange, watery, *gloop-gloop*ing noise filled the room. I frowned, then realized it must be the underwater microphones out in the bay, the same ones Uncle Joe was listening to. The noise felt thick in the air, heavy and heaving through the crackly old equipment. I listened, staring into space. It was seriously hypnotic.

I shook myself, switched off the machine, and looked around for something better to distract me.

And there was Fort Orpheus, filling the room. I glared at it, and an interesting new idea crept into my brain: What if I just tore it down? What if I yanked off the sheet, scattered the pillows, and drowned the postcard token out in the bay? What would happen then?

I'd be stuck, that's what would happen. I'd be trapped in Alaska with Uncle Joe, and right then that didn't sound bad at all. We could hang out together for the rest of the summer, just the two of us, and I could learn about whales and help Uncle Joe with his research. We would make double-strength cocoa every night after dinner and have huge bonfires on the beach, and when Orpheus showed up we would publish our findings and the two of us would become famous.

And as for Abby? She could keep Camp Pillow Fort, keep

NAFAFA and the links and all the rest of it. She could clean up that alley and take my spot on the Council and go around in fancy silver sunglasses, making her own banner and linking in all her Camp Cantaloupe friends and bossing around every west coast kid unlucky enough to discover a magical pillow fort from then on.

Uncle Joe and I would be famous and happy and better off without her.

Only, of course, that's not how things would really go. If I did get trapped in Alaska, then Uncle Joe would have to tell my mom I was there, and she would have to buy an expensive ticket to get me home. And Orpheus would probably turn up while Uncle Joe was driving me to the airport, then disappear forever. And Kelly would probably take a turn for the worse while my mom was coming to pick me up. And Abby would never forgive me and would convince her dad to move and I'd never see her again, and no one would ever speak to me in middle school, and . . .

I blinked, pulling myself out of the tragedy running in my head. Whoa. I was doing exactly what Abby had said. And if she'd been right about that . . .

Okay, fine, I was doing the thing, but that was just me being me, right? It's not like I was acting on it. I was just planning what I'd do if it *did* happen. Getting prepared. Trying it on for size.

My stomach gave a rumble, and I turned my back on the

fort and went to root around in the kitchen. It was all too much to deal with right then. At least making lunch would keep me busy for a bit.

There wasn't much to see in the cupboards, just canned soup, plain crackers, and some mismatched dishes. The fridge was worse, with only a carton of coffee creamer, half a jar of applesauce, and a lonely bottle of mustard wobbling all by itself in the door.

"Hey there," I said, waving at the mustard. "I know how you feel."

My heart twinged as I eyed the uninspiring collection of food. Poor Uncle Joe. Imagine coming in out of the cold and facing this. He'd been really nice about Abby and me hanging around and tearing up his living room, and he'd made us lunch on our first surprise visit. It was time I actually did something nice for him. Luckily the thing to do was obvious.

"Begin Operation Fridge Fix," I announced to the empty kitchen.

Five minutes and one first-class raid on my own fridge later I was back with a block of Cheddar, a loaf of bread, a jar of pickles, a half-full bottle of ranch dressing, a package of bacon, six cups of blueberry yogurt, seven apples, and a box of cherry Popsicles.

I was heading back for another round of kitchen pillaging when I bumped into Samson in my fort, nosing around near the link that led to Kelly's.

"Oh, no, not you," I said. Samson was my favorite cat in the world, but I was still angry and hurt over his owner. "You need to get back home now, buddy."

Samson and his snagglepaw took some convincing, and in the struggle I squashed an elbow into one of the unlinked wall pillows. It toppled, and I suddenly found myself face-to-face with a green, cracked, leathery-looking pillow that definitely wasn't one of mine.

"Ugh, really?" I groaned to the empty fort. "Again?"

EIGHTEEN

So there had been a second secret link all along? That would explain another of the mysterious lumps on NAFAFA's map of Camp Pillow Fort. I stared at it.

The new pillow was sitting one to the left of Kelly's. If Abby had started her search the other day going the opposite direction, we would have found this one first. And then where would we be? Maybe Abby and I wouldn't be fighting. Maybe I wouldn't feel so bad right now. Maybe I wouldn't be alone.

It was too late for maybes, though. Abby *had* gone the other way, charging off on her own like always, and here I was, and— Hey, you know what? She wasn't the only one who could go charging into things. Maybe it was my turn.

I shoved the pillow, hard, sending it flying into the

mystery fort. Bright light and bouncy electronic music streamed into Fort McForterson. I had a split second of triumph before the yell hit me.

"What the—!"

Oh, good. Someone was home.

Feeling gloriously reckless, I pushed my head and shoulders through the gap and looked around.

I was in a bedroom. A teenager's bedroom, judging by the band posters and the clothes on the floor. Oh, and Caitlin my across-the-street-neighbor jumping up from a desk right in front of me.

I froze, assessing the situation. My lower half was still back in Fort McForterson, and my upper half was sticking out of a green fake-leather love seat with laundry piled on it. The pillow I'd punched was standing on one side, holding a sheet like a roof over my head. I didn't see any sign of an organized pillow fort. This must have been one of those accidental forts, like Noriko had talked about in her letter.

I looked at Caitlin. She looked at me. The bouncy electronic music thumped along on its own. And then . . .

"Ha! I knew it!" Caitlin slapped the desk. "I freaking knew it!"

"Hi," I said. What was she talking about? How was that a proper reply to someone bursting out of your sofa? "You're, uh, probably surprised to see me."

"Nope."

"Nope?"

Caitlin shook her head. "I knew you were having awesome adventures this summer, Maggie. I told you so, remember?"

My brain felt just like the rest of me: only halfway there. "Kind of," I said, thinking back to when I rescued Samson from the banner on her ice cream truck. It felt like years ago.

Caitlin came over and plopped down on the floor. "So, someone finally started a west coast network, then?" she said.

The world as I knew it went up, down, inside out, and sideways. *Caitlin knew about the pillow fort networks? Caitlin? Then again, why not? In a world where Abby could walk out on me, anything was possible.*

"Yeah," I said, scraping together my remaining bits of reality. "I did. We did. But how do *you* know about that?"

"I moved here from Wisconsin when I was ten," said Caitlin. "Before the move I was in the Great Plains Sofa Circle." *Holy pickle jar, she really did know about NAFAFA.* "But when my network found out where I was going, they made me leave my token behind. I was cut off."

"Why didn't they let you just link back there from here?" Look at me, casually talking pillow fort theory with a high schooler.

"Oh, I argued for that, but my network head said it was against the rules to build a satellite fort in unclaimed territory, and if I tried to smuggle in a token and link in, they would shut me down anyway."

"Huh. Seems like they're always doing that."

"Right? But now tell me everything. You really started your own homegrown network out here?"

"Yup. Noriko—she's head of the Council right now—told us we're the only kids on the west coast to ever have a network." I couldn't keep a curl of pride out of my voice. "It's pretty cool being first. I just can't believe other kids never found scraps of the First Sofa and built pillow forts before us."

Caitlin quirked an eyebrow. "Oh, they totally did."

"What?"

"I don't know what this Noriko person told you, but my old network head told me all about it while I was trying to convince her to let me stay linked in. She said linkable forts have been popping up here and there on the west coast ever since the gold rush."

"The gold rush? Seriously?"

"Sure," said Caitlin. "It makes sense. A whole bunch of people moved west for that, bringing their pillows and blankets and things along. Their kids either came with them or showed up later, and ever since then some random kid on the west coast occasionally builds a fort that can be linked."

"But—but Noriko and Murray both specifically said we were a special case. They told us we were the first functioning network on the west coast, ever."

"Okay, then that's the key right there," said Caitlin, pointing. "The first *functioning* network. None of the forts I'm talking about ever actually got linked to others. My old head said accidentally getting the right pieces in place in one fort is hard enough. But having other forts close enough for that fort to start linking and form a network is almost impossible."

"Wow," I said. "So Abby and I did the impossible."

"Looks like," said Caitlin, smiling. "Good for you. But speaking of your amazing bestie, where is she? Why are you here all on your own?"

Oh, that.

Discovering the secret link to Caitlin had almost driven my other problems out of my mind. Now it all came flooding back and then some, along with the ache in my chest.

Caitlin leaned against the sofa as I explained the situation. "Ouch, that sounds really hard," she said when I finished. "I hope you two can patch it up soon."

I nodded. "Me too." And I meant it. I hated being mad at Abby. And I really hated knowing she was mad at me.

"Would a Mega Ultra Caramel Swizzle Cone help?" Caitlin asked. "I can run out to the truck."

"No!" called a voice from Fort McForterson, and I jumped as well as I could as someone behind me whapped me on the leg.

"Let me in," said the voice. It was a girl, but it definitely didn't sound like Abby. I scooched over, and first a baseball cap, then a bunch of curly black hair appeared.

"Carolina?"

"Oof." Carolina squeezed in beside me and looked around grumpily. "Hello, Maggie Hetzger," she said. "And hello person named Caitlin who shouldn't be linked in."

"Hi!" said Caitlin. "Nice to meet you. What network are you with? Do you want some ice cream?"

"I'm not here to make friends," said Carolina.

"She's with the Forts of the Eastern Seaboard," I told Caitlin.

"Ooo!" Caitlin smiled. "Fancy!"

"Stop it, stop it, stop it," said Carolina, waving her hands. "There's no time. You need to get back to your own network, Maggie Hetzger. This fort was accidental and it's not approved, and my surveillance shift is almost up. If the next kid catches you in here with a teenager, you'll be cut off permanently, and then some."

"Aw, that's what happened to me, sort of," said Caitlin. "It's not fun. You should get going."

"I guess so." It had been nice getting to talk things over with someone who mostly understood. "Can I come by again sometime?"

"No!" cut in Carolina. "This link shouldn't even be here. Caitlin's not allowed to be connected to any fort networks at all."

"That's true," said Caitlin. "We can hang out the normal way though, Maggie."

"Really? Thanks!"

Carolina was digging furiously through the jeans and skirts and shirts covering the floor around us.

"What are you doing?" I asked.

"Looking for the token."

Caitlin raised her eyebrows. "I didn't even ask how we got linked up! What do you think it was, Maggie? I mean, I gave you the ice cream, and your mail you dropped, but none of that would do it."

"Got it!" cried Carolina, emerging from the clothes pile with a cheap plastic pen in her hand.

"Ha!" I said. It was my old hypno-ray gun. "I forgot I even gave that to you."

"Same," said Caitlin. "And look how far you've come since then." We high-fived.

"Time to go, Maggie Hetzger," said Carolina.

"Bye, Caitlin," I said, scooching back to my own fort. "Thanks for everything."

"Go get 'em, tiger!" she called, waving.

I waited in Fort McForterson as Carolina pulled the link shut behind her.

"That was close," she said, tossing the pen back in my arts-and-crafts corner. She turned to me. "I know things are weird between you and Abby Hernandez right now, and that you're attempting a good deed on your own, but please, Maggie Hetzger, try and stay out of trouble."

Huh. So she knew about the fight. "You don't miss anything, do you?" I said.

Carolina shook her head. "It's my job." A smile snuck into the corners of her mouth. "Plus I'm training to be the world's greatest secret agent someday."

"Oh!" I said, sitting up. "Oh oh oh! Me too! That is awesome! We need to talk more about that." Maybe she could become my new Abby, if things, well, never got back to normal.

It was always good to be prepared for the worst.

Carolina shrugged. "Follow the rules, get into NAFAFA, and maybe we can. But now I have to go." She yanked a random pillow down, and there was the Hub again. "Good luck, Maggie Hetzger."

"Bye," I said. "And thank you."

I returned to Alaska. As I crawled out of Fort Orpheus, I realized I was actually feeling better. Hanging out with Caitlin and Carolina had really cheered me up.

I headed back to the kitchen and wolfed down a yogurt, admiring my work on Operation Fridge Fix. The fridge really did look a hundred times better, and I couldn't wait for Uncle Joe to see it. I went to the window to find him.

The weather had taken a turn for the worse. A steady rain was falling, and the wind was kicking up serious whitecaps out on the bay, but Uncle Joe was still out there, lying on the rocks by the shore. Why hadn't he come in? He must have been getting soaked. A kernel of worry dropped into my stomach, and I pulled on a sweater and rain jacket and headed out to check on him.

"Hey," I called, clomping down the steps. "Uncle Joe!" The wet wind threw the words right back at me.

I crunched over the beach. "Are you okay?" I hollered. The cold rain pattered on the hood of my jacket. Uncle Joe didn't look up. Why wasn't he answering? And hey, why was all his recording equipment still set up unprotected on the rocks around him?

Wait. It wasn't set up. It was tumbled, scattered.

I broke into a run, my shoes slipping on the stones, and then I saw his leg, bent out at an ugly angle, and I saw the rain running down his face.

His eyes were closed. My heart stopped.

He wasn't . . . he couldn't be . . .

I dropped down beside him, my fingers squeezing around his arm, and saw a faint cloud rise from his mouth before the wind whipped it away. I gasped with relief. He was alive, at least, but he was out cold and seriously hurt, and . . .

Oh. My. Cantaloupe.

He'd been like this the whole time. While I'd been moping around the cabin, fussing with the fridge, and chatting
with Carolina and Caitlin, Uncle Joe had been out here in the
freezing rain, desperately needing my help.

Forget being left behind from summer camp. Forget
fighting with my best friend.

I'd never felt worse in my life.

But what now? There was no way I could carry him back
to the cabin by myself, and I couldn't risk dragging him over
the rocks and making his injuries worse. I hugged my arms
around my jacket and scanned the icy hills and sky and bay,
fighting off a rising panic.

I couldn't save him on my own. I needed help. But my
go-to help was busy cleaning a dirty alleyway back in Seattle
and might not be speaking to me.

I sighed. This was going to be rough, and I was definitely
going to have to apologize first, but there was no way around
it. I covered Uncle Joe with my sweater and rain jacket and
ran shivering back to the cabin. It was time to rally the troops.

NINETEEN

The afternoon sun was already sliding down the far side of the sky, and all the heat of the day seemed to have crammed itself into the narrow alley behind the dump. It was swelteringly hot. It was also incredibly filthy, packed with overstuffed garbage bags, old paint cans, rotting food, ten million flies, and Abby, looking tired and grumpy as she pushed at a pile of plastic bottles and cardboard with a broom.

"Oh, look who decided to turn up," she said as I struggled out of the disgusting sofa. "What an honor."

I bit back a retort, thinking of Uncle Joe lying on the cold ground up in Alaska. I couldn't rescue him alone.

"Hi," I said. "I'm not here to help, I—"

"Oh, peachy," Abby said, dropping her broom and picking up a shovel. Her fancy braid was fraying at the end. "You're not here to help. Well, thank you very much for the visit, Ms. Vice Director." She kicked a tin can at the Dumpster against the wall. It struck with a clang, and a huge hairy something came streaking out from under it and disappeared behind the sofa.

"That's the rat, by the way," said Abby. "There is one. I named it Mr. Chompers. If you screw your eyes up really tight he almost looks like a moose."

"Great. Abby—"

"I keep thinking about what I would do if he actually turned into one and rescued me back to Camp Cantaloupe." She stabbed the shovel into the pile at her feet.

"Abby—"

"It could happen, you know? I never saw it at camp, so I think the moose owes me, and—"

"Oh, will you shut up about that moose and just let me apologize?!"

It wasn't how I meant to say it, but there it was. Abby whirled to face me, looking furious, but I charged ahead. "Look, I'm sorry for what I said before, and for trying to control everything, and for treating you like a sidekick and all the rest of it. You were right. I get it, and I'm sorry." I realized I was almost shouting. "I'm here because I need *your* help. Uncle Joe is hurt. He fell down on the beach and I'm pretty sure he has a broken leg."

The anger slid from Abby's face. She peered at me. "Is this another one of your games?"

I shook my head.

"He's really hurt?"

"Yes! He's collapsed on the rocks in the rain, unconscious."

"Unconscious?!" Abby's shovel clattered to the ground. "We have to rescue him!"

"Why do you think I'm here?" I said, but she was already racing for the sofa.

Okay. That went better than I'd expected.

"So, what's your plan?" asked Abby as I crowded after her into Fort McForterson.

"Well, first we need to get him inside," I said. "And then we'll just have to—"

"Wait, wait-wait-wait-wait," said Abby. "Are you serious? If Joe's really hurt, there's no way we can do this on our own. We need to get my dad or someone. We need an adult."

"You know we can't bring grown-ups in," I said. "It's against NAFAFA rules. They'll shut us down and then Uncle Joe will be trapped up there without any help at all."

"But this is a real emergency," said Abby. "And— Hey! Didn't Noriko say—" She cleared her throat and looked up at the blanket ceiling. "Okay, so we, the members of Camp Pillow Fort, are hereby declaring a genuine, actual, medical emergency. Yes."

"What are you doing?"

"Telling the Council. Noriko said we could only break the rules for *life-or-death emergencies*, and this should definitely count."

"Brilliant," I said, wishing I'd thought of it. "That changes things. So where can we find—"

We both jumped as the pillow to Fort Comfy flopped open.

"Oh, honestly, Samson," said Abby as the cat ambled in. "You always have to make an entrance, don't you?"

Samson danced around happily, dodging Abby's hands and getting caught on everything until he came to the link to the alley fort. He stopped dead, sniffing furiously, and dropped into a crouch.

"Huh," said Abby. "Maybe he smells Mr. Chompers."

"He definitely smells something," I said as Samson began pawing at the pillow.

Abby grabbed him around the middle. "All right, time to go home, Mr. Director. No rat fights allowed in other people's forts."

But Samson wasn't in the mood to be grabbed.

"Stop squirming," said Abby. "We've got an emergency here, buddy. Ow! Hey!"

"Can I help?" I asked.

"No, I got this. He's just stuck on— Ow!"

"Abby? You okay?" said a new voice.

We froze. Abby's head snapped up.

It was one of her brothers.

"I'm fine!" she yelled, throwing herself into the open link, Samson twisting in her arms. "Don't come in—"

But there was a swoosh of fabric and a whoosh of air, and Mark's head and shoulders appeared in the entrance to Fort Comfy, the tassels of Abby's scarf brushing his face.

He looked at Abby, then past her to the open link.

He blinked. He frowned. He turned his head.

"Hey, Matt!" he yelled. "Get in here!"

"No!" said Abby, but it was too late. There was a pounding of footsteps and Matt appeared, squeezing his way in next to Mark. He blinked and frowned just like his brother, then settled on an identical openmouthed stare. They looked adorable.

Abby went on the offensive.

"What do you think you're doing?!" she demanded, unhooking Samson from her shirt. "How dare you come in my fort without permission?"

"You yelled," said Mark. "But what's going on here?"

"Nothing," said Abby firmly. I didn't move a muscle. Maybe Abby could talk her way out of this. Maybe they would forget what they'd seen.

Matt, peering over Abby's shoulder, crinkled his eyebrows at me through the link. "Really?" he said. "'Cause this sure looks like something to me." He tilted his head at me and waved. I couldn't help it—I waved back.

"Ugh!" Abby heaved a dramatic sigh. "Come on, then," she said, and she backed up into Fort McForterson to sit beside me. Matt and Mark squeezed through Fort Comfy and piled together in the link, Mark on his stomach with Matt leaning on his shoulders. They were so close I could have reached out and ruffled Matt's hair. It was hard not to.

"So why are you two checking on me?" asked Abby, glaring at her brothers. "Where's Dad?"

"First tell us what's going on here," said Mark.

Abby gave an actual *tsk*-sigh. "You guys, it's fine. It's just this thing. Magic pillow forts or whatever. Get over it. So, where's Dad?"

Matt grinned at her. "Thanks. Dad's out on a date with Tamal. He won't be home until late. He left us in charge since you're grounded."

"And I heard you yelling," said Mark. "So I came to make sure you were okay."

"So here we are," said Matt.

"Yes," said Abby. "And it's nice to see you, but Maggie and I are in a hurry. We're on a rescue mission, and unless one of you knows how to heal broken bones—"

"Broken bones?" said Mark.

"Who's got broken bones?" asked Matt.

"No one you know."

"Oh, okay," said Mark. "So, what's our plan?"

"Are you asking if you can help?" said Abby. "Because you're not exactly in charge here."

"They can help," I said.

"They can?" said Abby.

"Yeah." With the news that Alex wasn't around, an idea was coming together in my mind. There really was only one obvious solution. It was time to be decisive.

"Okay, everyone!" I said, clapping my hands. "Here's what we're doing. Matt and Mark—"

But my explanation got cut off as a pillow popped out of the wall beside me and a young kid I'd never seen in my life appeared, silhouetted in the light and bustle of the NAFAFA Hub.

"Maggie Hetzger?" said the kid, reading from a clipboard.

"Pheasant!" I snapped, raising my hand. Abby snorted.

The kid looked up. "Ben from the Council would like to know if this is actually a true, legitimate emergency."

I could have screamed in frustration. I might have.

"YES," I said, snatching up the loose pillow and strangling it. "What is wrong with you people? This is a real, actual, life-and-death emergency, and we are dealing with it whether anyone on that darn Council likes it or not!" The boy looked shocked. He almost dropped his clipboard.

"And you tell Ben from me," I barreled on, closing the

distance between us, "that if he shuts down one single link in this network before Uncle Joe is safe, I will catch the next bus to the Midwest and search under every pillow on every sofa until I find him. And he will not be pleased to see me!" And I slammed the link shut in his face.

"Ugh," I said, turning back to the others.

Abby was goggling at me. Mark whistled. Even Samson looked impressed.

"Guess we know who's in charge around here, then," said Matt, grinning.

I felt my face turn scarlet. "So, like I was saying," I said. "Matt and Mark, you two go up to Alaska and stand guard over Uncle Joe. We'll tell you how to get there."

"Got it," said Matt.

"When you say Alaska . . . ," began Mark, but Abby put her hand in the air.

"What about me?" she asked.

I looked at her. Things had been really weird between us, but this next stage was going to be tricky, and I needed her brains and bravery and friendship more than ever.

"We," I said, "are going through to Kelly's fort, Abs. We're going to get my mom."

TWENTY

Kelly had made some changes to her fort since the makeover. The little table had been moved to the center, and it was covered with crayons, pens, and half-finished drawings instead of our random knickknacks, which were dumped in the old basket. Abby pointed to one of the drawings-in-progress and grinned: a group of cats in a pillow fort on the moon, roasting marshmallows over a candle.

We waited, listening for movement on the other side of the blanket, but everything seemed quiet. Abby crept out of the fort.

"Hi!" said a cheery voice. "Are you my magical pen pal?"

I jumped, nearly knocking over the table, and peeked out. Kelly was sitting up in bed. It looked like she'd been waiting for us.

Abby kept her cool.

"Yes to the second part, no to the first," she said, getting to her feet. "I'm not magical, although the forts might be; no one's really sure. My name's Abby."

"I'm Kelly." They shook hands. "I finished your picture." Kelly held up a drawing of a black-and-white cat floating happily through space. It looked almost exactly nothing like Samson.

Abby smiled. "Aww! I love it, thanks."

"You're welcome. Are the other people here?"

"Yup," said Abby, waving for me to come out. "This is Maggie. She's the other people."

"Hello," I said.

"Hi!" Kelly didn't seem even the tiniest bit nervous to be meeting two new kids, older kids even, who had just crawled out of her personal, private pillow fort. I was impressed.

"So, we're in a hurry, Kelly," said Abby, sitting on the bed, "but we owe you an explanation for what's been going on. Here's the one-minute version. . . ."

Abby told Kelly everything: building the forts, discovering the links, Alaska, the Council, the attack, how our parents reacted—all of it. Kelly listened, her eyes growing wider and wider.

"And Dr. Hetzger," she said, turning to me when Abby was finished, "she's your *mom*? Weird!"

"Not that weird," I said. "Your fort's linked in because my mom took some crimping scissors from my fort and gave them to you."

"Oh, those are yours?" said Kelly. "Do you want them back?"

"No, thanks," I said. "They were actually my mom's, but they're yours now. They're your token."

"If we took those scissors out of your fort, we wouldn't be able to visit you at all anymore," explained Abby. "It's having the scissors here that makes it possible. That's what 'token' means."

"This is all pretty confusing," said Kelly.

"It is," agreed Abby, "and if you want, we can go over all of it again once we rescue Maggie's uncle Joe."

"And Uncle Joe needs a doctor," I said, walking over to the door, "which is why we're here to get my mom."

I had my hand on the doorknob when Kelly shouted.

"Stop!" she said. "You can't go out there. You don't know where she is. You'll get in trouble with the doctors."

"Ooh! She's right, Mags," said Abby. "There are probably lots of grown-ups wandering around, and we're not exactly supposed to be here."

"But we have to find her," I insisted. I was getting more and more anxious by the second. How long had it been since I'd left Uncle Joe all on his own? We'd been wasting time.

"And we will," said Abby. "But we need a plan."

"What about this?" Kelly pulled a push button on a cord off the wall beside her. "It's my emergency button. I'm only supposed to use it for big emergencies, but this probably counts. Dr. Hetzger should be who answers it."

"Perfect!" said Abby. "You're good at plans, Kelly. But what should we say when she shows up? How are we going to convince her to get in the fort?"

"We'll just have to wing it," I said. "We've got to do this. Ready?"

Kelly grinned and pressed the emergency button.

Twelve seconds later my mom burst through the door.

"Kelly? What is— MAGGIE?!" She goggled, spinning from me, to Kelly holding the emergency button, to Abby, who waved, and back to me again. "What do you think you're doing here? You're supposed to be at home. You're supposed to be grounded!" I opened my mouth, but she cut me off. "No, never mind, you can explain later." She crossed to the bed and put a hand on Kelly's shoulder. "I'm so sorry about this, Kelly, but I'm proud of you for using the button and calling for help."

"I wasn't calling for help," said Kelly.

"You weren't?"

"No," said Kelly. "I pressed the button so you'd come to Alaska with us."

I looked at Abby in surprise. When did we say Kelly was coming with us? Apparently she had some plans of her own.

"That sounds like a nice game," said my mom. "But this isn't a good time for games."

"It's not a game, Ms. H.," said Abby.

My mom's jaw tightened. "That is enough, Abigail. You two are going to leave, now, and Kelly is going to get some rest, and there's nothing more to say."

"What if I do this?" said Kelly, and she jumped out of bed.

"Hey!" said my mom as Kelly shoved her feet into a pair of hospital slippers and pattered over to the fort. Abby whooped. I shook my head. This little girl had some serious nerve, and if she felt well enough to decide she was going to come along, I wasn't going to stop her.

"Head through the link, Kelly," I called as she disappeared into the entrance. "Then take the second pillow to the right and straight on to Alaska."

"Stop it!" said my mom, crossing to the fort. "Kelly, come out of there, sweetie. You can play in your fort later."

There was no reply.

"She's not in there anymore," said Abby. "We told you— she's on her way to Alaska."

"I said stop it! This is absolutely not a game, girls!" My mom looked more upset than I'd ever seen her. She ducked inside the fort.

"Get the door!" hissed Abby, following my mom. I bolted for the door and locked it, turning off the lights for good measure, and scrambled after them just as my mom cried out.

"Holy— What?! What is this?"

"Hey, keep it moving, Ms. H," said Abby, bumping into her from behind. "Just follow the open links."

We crowded into Fort McForterson just in time to hear Kelly say, "Whee!" as she tumbled through the pillow to Uncle Joe's. My mom stopped dead and stared around open-mouthed.

"But this is your—our— We're in—"

"Yes, yes," I said. "It's the fort in our living room, but right now we're heading to Uncle Joe's place up in Alaska. He needs our help."

"Joe . . . ?"

"Joe, your little brother, yes. Oh come *on*, Mom!"

Coaxing and tugging, we finally got my mom through the forts, past the stomach-churning link, and out into Uncle Joe's cabin, where Kelly was running out the front door in her bathrobe and slippers.

"Kelly, wait! You'll freeze!" I called.

"I'm on it!" said Abby, pulling a pair of jackets from the closet and running after her. I turned to my mom. Her eyes were spinning between the fort and the cabin and the wind-swept tundra outside. She looked completely bewildered. I grabbed her shoulders with both hands and prepared to take control of the situation.

"Mom," I said, "I know this is confusing, but take a deep, slow breath, remember? I need you to listen to me."

We both looked around as heavy feet thudded up the front steps, and Matt came tromping in.

"About time!" he said. "It stopped raining, but he's still out cold."

"Wha—? What are you doing here?" said my mom.

"The same as you, Ms. H. Rescue mission."

"But, but . . . ," my mom sputtered.

"Mom!" I was worried I would have to slap her face, but her eyes locked onto me like I was holding out a lifeline. "Mom, we're in Uncle Joe's cabin in Alaska. I found him out on the shore a little while ago, unconscious and hurt. He needs your help."

Her eyes were scanning side to side as I spoke.

"Joe . . . what? But how—?"

"There's no time to explain, but my friends and I can travel between our pillow forts and that's how we got here, and this is an emergency, so follow me!"

I pulled her to the door, Matt right behind us. She gasped as the cold air hit her and stopped, staring out at the arctic sky and waves and shore. I was already running down the steps.

"Straight ahead!" I called over my shoulder. And then my mom saw them: Abby, Mark, and Kelly gathered around the crumpled heap that was Uncle Joe. She gave a cry, and before I could take another two steps she was sprinting past me, a blur in her purple hospital scrubs, tearing across the rain-slicked rocks to rescue her little brother.

TWENTY-ONE

"Have you moved him at all?" my mom asked, crouching down beside Uncle Joe and pressing a hand to his face.

"No," said Mark as Matt and I jogged up. "We thought that wouldn't be safe."

My mom ran her hands gingerly along Uncle Joe's twisted leg, then exhaled hard and turned to us, her face pale but relieved.

"You did the right thing; it's a nasty break. The good news is that otherwise he doesn't seem to be in danger."

Abby spun and flung her arms around me. Matt and Mark gave a cheer. I squeezed Abby back and exhaled hard into the sky as the cloud of worry and anxiety that had been hovering over us lifted.

My mom climbed to her feet. "Okay, everyone," she said,

clapping her hands. "Here's what we're doing: our number one priority is to get Joe warm, so we need to carry him inside. Gather around and we'll lift him together. I'll keep his leg stable until we can get a splint on it."

Everybody helped, and with a good amount of slipping and straining we managed to haul Uncle Joe back into the cabin and onto the bed. My mom carefully positioned his leg, then clapped her hands again and gave us all chores: Kelly and Abby went to gather up all the blankets and warm things they could find; Matt and Mark rooted through the cupboards looking for medical supplies; and I boiled water on the stove and make six giant mugs of hot cocoa.

And even though it was still technically an emergency, it was also pretty fun, with all of us crammed together in the tiny cabin gulping cocoa, digging through drawers and boxes for useful supplies, and shouting when we found them. Abby found a local map under a heavy book on whale anatomy, Kelly discovered a stash of extra blankets at the back of the closet, and Matt pulled a pair of ski poles out from under the bed that my mom decided would be perfect for splints.

Amid all the searching someone bumped the electronic clutter on the desk, and after a few sputtering crackles the same weird, heavy, soupy, staticy noise I'd heard before began churning into the room. Everyone stopped what they were doing to stare at the speaker.

"I'm pretty sure that's the underwater microphone," I told them.

"It's incredible," whispered Matt. Mark nodded.

"Where are the whales, though?" asked Kelly. No one answered, and we listened in silence to the gurgling, glooping thunder of the deep, dark water out in the bay.

There was a groan from the bed, and the spell was broken.

"He's waking up!"

We all crowded around as Uncle Joe opened his eyes. He looked from one face to another, blinking in the light.

"Joe," said my mom, "Joe, it's me, Karen. You had a bad fall. You've got a broken leg and probably a concussion."

"Hey, Sis," said Uncle Joe faintly. "Nice to see you, too."

"How are you feeling?" I asked, leaning over him.

"Hurt," said Uncle Joe. "Who are you?"

I looked at my mom in alarm.

"I'm Maggie, your niece. . . ."

"Not you, Maggie, *you*." He nodded, then grimaced. "Ouch, guess I shouldn't do that."

I looked over my shoulder. Kelly and the twins were standing behind me.

"Oh, these are friends of ours," I said. "This is Kelly. She's—"

But Uncle Joe's face spasmed, and he gritted his teeth around another groan.

"The shock's wearing off," said my mom, laying a hand

on his forehead. "He's starting to feel that broken leg. Okay, Joe, we're going to get you to the hospital."

"Which—hospital?"

"Mine," said my mom. "Through the pillow forts."

It was incredibly bizarre hearing my mom say those words, but everyone took it in stride. Everyone, that it, except Uncle Joe, who shook his head again.

"Ouch!" he said. "La-la! Don't tell—me—anything! And can't leave Alaska—lose grant. Have to stay—send reports—be ready—record whale."

"Joe, that's enough," said my mom. "We're taking you to the hospital and that's that. You're in no position to argue."

"Your mom sounds just like you," Abby whispered, nudging me.

Uncle Joe frowned and opened his mouth, clearly ready to put up a fight, then grimaced again and shut it. He was trembling.

"Are you in a lot of pain?" asked Kelly. He gave a tiny nod. She patted his arm. Then her eyes lit up. "Oh! Dr. Hetzger!"

"Yes, Kelly?"

"Why don't we get Joe some emergency pain medicine, like you keep in my room? I can run and get it for him."

"It's kind of you to think of that," said my mom. "But seeing as we're taking him there in a minute anyway—"

"No!" said Uncle Joe. "Hospital—here. Town not—too far."

"He wants to stay, Ms. H.," said Matt.

"Stop. It's not safe, kids."

"But shouldn't he get a say?" asked Abby. "He's the one who's injured."

"We'd have a seriously hard time getting him through all those links while he's like this, anyway," Mark pointed out.

My mom bit her lip, considering.

Kelly tugged at her sleeve. "I think he's really hurting, Dr. Hetzger."

My mom gave in. "Fine," she said, throwing up her hands. "We'll take Joe to this town hospital. But *I'll* go get the pain medicine from mine."

"Do you want help getting back there?" I asked. The last thing we needed was my mom getting lost in the network.

"I remember. I'll just follow the open links like you said." She disappeared into the fort, and we waited for an anxious minute before she returned. "Here," she said, holding out a small plastic bottle. "I'm not happy about this, but these will help Joe for now."

"Thank—goodness," said Uncle Joe. I ran to get a glass of water.

"Great idea, Kelly," said Abby as I helped Uncle Joe with the medicine. "Now, how exactly are we going to get Joe to his hospital?"

"Why don't we take this truck out back?" called Mark, pointing out the kitchen window. "Does it run okay, Joe?"

Uncle Joe, breathing shallowly, gave a thumbs-up.

"Cool, looks like we've got a plan, then," said Matt. "I can drive. Is everybody— Whoa!"

He cut off as the entrance flap of Fort Orpheus billowed dramatically and Samson appeared, purring like a freight train at the sight of everyone, Creepy Frog dangling from his snagglepaw.

"Samson!" cried Abby. "The legend continues."

"Well, the gang's all here now," said Mark.

"So that's Samson," Kelly said, kneeling down to pet him. Samson rubbed her fingers with his cheek.

"Where did that cat come from?" asked my mom. "And what on earth is that thing he's dragging?"

"He's my cat," said Abby, freeing him from the stuffed animal. "He likes to wander through our network. And this is Creepy Frog."

"It certainly is," said my mom. "And Samson is very handsome, but we can't afford to get distracted right now."

But it was too late for that, as Abby chucked Creepy Frog at me, Samson got caught on Kelly's bathrobe, Matt and Mark started arguing over who was going to drive the truck, and I missed Creepy Frog and knocked over my cocoa.

Eventually we all settled down, but the plan hit a new snag as my mom tried to decide who was going to help deliver Uncle Joe to the hospital.

Obviously, everyone wanted to go.

"Absolutely not!" said my mom, shaking her head over

and over. "I am not taking you all on a nighttime joyride across the Alaskan tundra. It would be wildly irresponsible of me, both as a parent and a doctor."

"But we can't just go home," I said. "Not after everything we've done!"

"Oh, yes, you can," she retorted. "And as the only uninjured adult here, I'm ordering you and Abby back home immediately and Kelly back to the hospital. Matt and Mark," she said, speaking over our objections, "will ride in the bed of the truck and look after Joe while I drive."

"Sure, Ms. H.," said Matt. "But how are you going to know where to go? It's not safe to read a map and drive at the same time."

"I'll manage," said my mom. "Joe won't fit up front with his splint, and I need two people in the back to stop him from rolling around."

"Maggie and I can do that," said Abby, her hand in the air. "We can keep him steady. That way the twins can ride up front with you and read the map, and if anything goes wrong in back I can handle it because I learned all about first aid and stuff at Camp Cantaloupe."

My mom wasn't convinced.

"Kids, this is a very, very important thing we're about to do. Joe needs serious medical attention, and I'd be better able to help him if I knew you were all safely at home."

"We can do it, Ms. H.," said Abby. "We want to help. Just give us a chance. Please."

My mom stared at her for a long moment, then sighed.

"Fine," she said. "But only because this is a real emergency."

"What about me?" asked Kelly.

I nodded. "Kelly has to come too."

"Whoa, whoa, whoa!" said my mom, raising her hands. "Who's the parent here?" Uncle Joe, who'd been keeping quiet, chuckled. "Kelly, no, you are absolutely not coming; it's just not safe. What if you caught a cold or developed a cough?"

"But I'll be with you," said Kelly. "What's safer than being with my doctor?"

"Being back in the hospital where you belong!" said my mom. She was turning red. "Okay, I don't know what I was thinking. I'm canceling this whole wild circus. Joe, you're coming back to my hospital with Kelly and me. The rest of you are going to help us carry Joe through the pillow forts, then get yourselves home and stay there. No argument, no discussion."

We'd only just started arguing and discussing when Uncle Joe sat halfway up and shouted, "Hey! Everybody quiet!"

In the ringing silence that followed, a long, sweet, ghostly noise filled the cabin, rising and falling like a bird on the air.

It was coming from the underwater speaker. The hair on the back of my neck stood up.

"What is that?" whispered the twins.

"Whale song," said Uncle Joe, his eyes wide. "It's Orpheus. He's here! You!" He pointed to Mark. "Hit Record on the receiver! Quick!"

Mark scrambled over to the table and pressed a button on the ancient machine. Uncle Joe let out a breath and lay back.

"Oh, wow, finally! You have no idea how cool— Might be the first people to ever hear this."

The song coiled around us, eerie and beautiful. I turned to look out the window, shivering at the thought of that huge, warm body slipping through the icy water just offshore.

"Orpheus . . . ," said Uncle Joe. "You're not alone, buddy." He looked like he might cry. He turned to my mom. "That settles it. I'm not going back to Seattle. I've waited my whole life for this moment."

My mom gazed around at our circle of rebellious faces. Samson hopped off the desk and crossed the room to sit daintily at Kelly's feet.

My mom sighed. "I suppose he's coming too, is he?" she said.

Samson purred.

TWENTY-TWO

It took another full half hour to gather ourselves together and actually get on the road.

The main problem was Uncle Joe, who flatly refused to leave while Orpheus was singing unless we could find some way to bring the radio. It was becoming a real argument when the twins found a set of official-looking walkie-talkies in the cutlery drawer in the kitchen.

"If we tape one handset down to TALK and set it near the speaker, you should be able to hear the radio for a few miles at least," said Matt. Uncle Joe was thrilled.

Soon the cocoa cups were piled in the sink, the back of the truck was toweled dry and loaded up with blankets, and we were carrying Uncle Joe awkwardly down the steps into the growing twilight. The wind was still going strong, roaring in off the bay and pushing the last of the clouds back to reveal a sky already twinkling with stars.

The twins settled Uncle Joe in the bed of the truck, and Kelly, Abby, Samson, and I piled in around him. My mom fussed over all of us, adjusting hats and tucking in blankets, then got behind the wheel as Mark climbed into the passenger seat and opened the map.

Matt ran back to the cabin to lock up and turn off the lights, then hopped over the tailgate beside Kelly.

"Wait," Abby said, jumping up from her seat beside me. "Here, take my spot."

"There's room on this side," said Matt.

"No," Abby insisted, stepping over Uncle Joe and cutting him off. "Not a chance, I want to sit next to Kelly and Samson. You sit next to Maggie."

I could have died, she was being so obvious, but no one else seemed to notice. I was incredibly grateful for the cold wind giving me an excuse to be pink in the face as Matt settled into the nest of blankets beside me. He took up more room than Abby. Our knees were almost touching. Oh, cantaloupe.

"Well, this is pretty sweet," Matt said, turning to me with a huge smile. "I get to ride with the lady in charge."

I smiled back as best I could and flatly refused to catch Abby's eye.

"Okay," said my mom, sliding open the little window

between the cab and the back of the truck. "All set back there?"

"Yes," we chorused.

"I have to go to the bathroom!" called Uncle Joe. My mom groaned. "Ha, just kidding."

Everyone laughed.

"Then if we're ready to act like grown-ups, here we go," said my mom. She turned the key, the engine roared to life, and we were off.

The icy arctic air whipped over us as the truck sped along, and I was instantly grateful for the mountain of coats and blankets my mom had insisted on bringing. Matt cinched the hood of his jacket tight and threw another blanket over our laps.

Abby leaned forward, patting Uncle Joe's arm. "How you hanging in there?" she hollered over the wind.

Uncle Joe gave a thumbs-up, waving the walkie-talkie.

Kelly was riding with her head thrown back, gazing up at the dark sky and gleaming stars from her little cocoon of warmth. Her eyes shone. I could just see Samson and Creepy Frog snuggled in her lap. She spotted me watching and waved. I grinned and waved back.

Up in the cab I saw Mark shake out the map and say something to my mom. She laughed, her ponytail bouncing. She looked happier than I'd seen her in a long time, and I felt a sudden rush of affection for her. Somehow, she actually fit in on this adventure. She made it complete.

Mark spread the map over the dashboard, studying it, then pointed to the left. My mom nodded and spun the wheel sharply, pointing the nose of the truck down as we curved around a line of hills.

Everyone in the back looked up at the turn, and everyone saw it, and everyone shouted, but it was too late. We were leaving the stars and the wind behind.

We were driving into a solid wall of fog.

* * *

There was no time to turn. The hills held the heavy gray cloud between them like a sea, and our path went right through it. Within seconds we were swallowed whole.

My mom slammed on the brakes, bringing the truck to a bouncing stop.

We stared around, but the fog threw the headlights back, reflecting only shining whiteness. The wind was gone, and the damp, clammy cold crept into the truck, finding every gap in our defenses. Abby pulled her hat down over her ears. Kelly disappeared completely under her blankets.

"I'm going to have to take this super slowly, everyone," my mom called from the front, easing the truck into a crawl. "There's no point trying to go back, but if we're lucky we'll come out of this soup soon."

Mark had the map inches from his face.

"It looks like we should be okay," he said. "This is only a sort of valley between the hills. Once we're through we won't be that far from town."

"But how long will it take to get through?" asked Matt. "At this speed it could be hours."

"We don't have a choice," said my mom. "We can't risk hitting something if we're going fast. Everybody just sit tight." She was doing her best to sound optimistic, but I could hear the worry in her voice. "How you doing back there, Joe?" she called.

"I'm okay, Sis," he called back. "I am okay." Now that we were moving quietly I could hear faint *sloop*s and *eeeow*s from the walkie-talkie. It looked like Orpheus was still singing.

"Well, keep it up," said my mom. "We'll be at the hospital before you know it."

We crawled forward, the only sound the crunch of the tires on the rocky ground and the occasional blip of whale song. On and on, and the fog got deeper. I felt a gnawing in my stomach, an uneasy mix of worry and plain old hunger. It had been a long time since I'd eaten. I wondered how the others were doing. Without the stars and the wind and the thrill of speed, our rescue mission was a lot less fun. No one was smiling now.

All sense of time slipped away. We might have been inching along for hours. I was starting to wonder if we were moving at all when Mark shouted in alarm and the truck stopped with a jolt.

"What the—?" said Abby, but looking ahead I could see exactly *what*. My mom had hit the brakes only just in time. The truck's front bumper was inches from a wall of rubble right across our path.

"Darn it!" said my mom. "There must have been a landslide." She hit the steering wheel in frustration, catching the horn with her fist. The tinny beep sounded small and forlorn in the shrouded landscape.

"Here there be margins," Abby said under her breath. I managed a weak smile.

"Can't we turn and follow alongside the slide?" asked Matt.

"We can try," said Mark, his head bent over the map. "But which way? The slide's right across our path, and there's no way of knowing if taking a left or right will get us around it faster."

My mom turned off the engine.

"Why stopped?" asked Uncle Joe sleepily. "Are we there?"

"No, Joe," said Abby. "Not yet. We're just taking a quick break."

Uncle Joe mumbled something unintelligible and closed his eyes.

"What do we do now?" asked Kelly in a small voice.

Nobody answered. I could feel Matt shivering beside me. The seconds ticked by. What *were* we going to do? We could always wait for day and hope the sun would burn away the fog, but how far off would that be? And what sort of condition would Uncle Joe—or any of us—be in when it came?

"Shame," mumbled Uncle Joe.

"What, Joe?" asked my mom.

Uncle Joe shook the walkie-talkie. "Out of batteries."

"Oh."

Silence fell over the group again. The silence grew. I could almost hear everybody thinking.

Finally, my mom spoke.

"Okay, what if we—"

"*Shh!*" hissed Abby. "What's that?"

We froze, listening, and I heard it: a steady crunching. The crunching of footsteps over the rocks. Something large, something . . . heavy . . . was moving out in the fog.

I sat up straight, my eyes wide and my ears trained on whatever was out there as it came nearer and nearer, circling, closing in on us. *Stalking*, said an unhelpful voice in my head. I shivered. It suddenly occurred to me how very exposed we were, sitting there in the open back of the truck, ready to be picked off one by one. . . .

There was a sharp crack of rock breaking, then a grumbling snort. What animal snapped rocks just by walking?

Maybe it was a woolly mammoth. Maybe it was the last woolly mammoth in the world, and it had been lost in the arctic, forced to become carnivorous to survive. Maybe it was sniffing us out, trying to decide which of us to yank into the air with its trunk and devour first.

Maybe it had settled on me. Maybe I was about to see the inside of a woolly mammoth's belly again, only this time without the pillows. I hoped I at least got a look at it first.

"There!" hissed Mark, pointing, and everyone gasped as an enormous shape appeared barely ten feet away, then vanished again into the mist.

"On the count of three," said my mom in a loud whisper, "I'm going to blow the horn. Maybe it'll go away." We all nodded. "One . . ." The crunching came closer. "Two . . ." There was a huffling, muffled snort. "Thr—"

"Wait!" said Matt. "Look!"

And it emerged out of the fog like a ship on the sea: dark eyes, a huge furry body, four massive legs, jaws that could crush us like grapes, and antlers, enormous antlers parting the mist before them. It came right up to the back of the truck and stopped.

It was a moose. A gargantuan moose of mammoth proportions. I'd always pictured moose as being kind of funny; but now, with one standing over me, its huffing nostrils adding to the fog and its antlers scraping the sky, the only word I could think of was *RUN*.

"Everyone," my mom said out of the side of her mouth, "keep very, very still."

We did. The moose stared down at us and blinked.

"Hey, Joe," breathed Abby. "What do we do?"

Uncle Joe gave a little snore. He was fast asleep.

"That thing could flip over the truck just by shaking its head, Ms. H.," whispered Mark. "We have to get out of here."

"I agree," my mom whispered back. "But how? I can't drive over this wall of rocks, and I can't back up with that thing standing there. We have to make it move somehow."

"Let's try and scare it," said Mark. "You honk the horn, and we'll hit it with something. What do we have that we can throw?"

"No, don't," I said. What were they all talking about? The moose wasn't hurting anybody—it was just standing there. As far as we knew, it could even be here to help us find our way out of the fog, like the ghost moose in those stories Abby brought home from Camp . . . Cantaloupe. . . .

I looked back up at our new friend, my heart thudding. But not from fear anymore.

"There's a toolbox in the back here," Matt said, fumbling under the blankets. He pulled out a solid-looking wrench and passed it through the window to Mark, then grabbed a hammer for himself.

"Okay, on three, you honk the horn, Ms. H., and we'll throw." He shared a grim nod with his brother. "Aim for between the eyes."

"Wait!" I said, horrified. "You can't! Abby, tell them."

Abby looked around, startled. "Huh? Tell them what?"

"That it's here to rescue us! It's obviously the ghost moose from Camp Cantaloupe." The moose coughed. "See?" I said. "It knows the name."

What I could see of Abby's forehead wrinkled. Her eyes traveled up to the moose, then back to me. "Mags, you know that was just a story, right?"

"But—you believed it. I know you did. You've barely stopped talking about it since you got back."

"Yeah, 'cause it's funny," said Abby. "And because I thought maybe you'd be into it, with your games and all, and maybe not be grumpy about me being gone. I didn't actually believe the ghost story part of it. Obviously."

"And even now there's an actual ghost moose standing over us"—I waved a hand at it—"an actual ghost moose as large as life, you still don't believe that it's real?"

Abby pulled her hat down over her eyebrows. "Mags, that doesn't even make sense," she said. "It's just a wild animal."

I looked around for support. Was I the only one who thought this moose might actually be a good thing? My mom was shaking her head. Mark wouldn't meet my eye. Matt quirked his mouth to one side and shrugged.

"Is it a friendly ghost moose?" asked a tiny voice from inside Kelly's cocoon.

"Yes," I said. "Thank you, Kelly, it's very friendly. That's how the story goes, anyway." I shot Abby a look. "It saves campers when they're lost in the woods."

Kelly peered out, her face just visible. "We're lost," she said.

She looked so small and hopeful in that moment that I couldn't stand it, and a hot spark of anger burned to life inside me. Who cared if it was just a story? Who cared if believing it didn't make any sense? This was what was happening. If I'd had my way, we'd have been rescued by a helicopter full of secret-agent librarians headed for their base in a nearby volcano. But the ghost moose of Camp Cantaloupe was what we got, and I'd eat a whole pan of cucumber casserole before I let this chance pass us by.

I smiled at Kelly, my heart fluttering a little at what I was about to do. "That's right," I said, putting my shoulders back. "We are. But not for long." The music started. I pushed my nest of blankets aside.

I stood up.

Everyone gasped.

The mist parted, billowing around me as I planted my feet, my head held high. I stood taller than the others, taller than the cab of the truck, taller than the hills around us, taller than the sky. The reflected headlights burned in the air like moonlight, and the vast arctic night stretched away on all sides. I raised my chin. The fog blew through my hair.

"Wow," someone breathed behind me.

I looked up at the moose. It gazed down, a puzzled sort of interest on its face.

For a ghost moose it sure did smell.

"Hello, hi," I said to it. What was the proper way to address a ghost moose? "If you're who I think you are and you're here from Camp Cantaloupe, will you please show us the way to town? We're lost, and Uncle Joe is hurt, and Kelly and my mom have to get back to the hospital, and Samson is probably hungry. And we could really use your help."

The moose stayed perfectly still, watching me, mist rolling down its antlers.

"So . . . please?" I said, my voice shaking slightly. "Will you help us?" I was starting to shiver. I'd been hoping for a grand, dramatic moment. This wasn't exactly going to plan.

The moose flicked one ear, then the other.

"Sweetie, I don't think . . . ," began my mom.

"*Shh,*" I said. I was thinking hard. The moose wasn't leaping to our aid, but it wasn't leaving, either. Maybe I wasn't doing enough on my own. Maybe the moose needed more. It was a pity we didn't have any cantaloupe lying around.

But Abby had said the moose helped lost campers. That was the story. And I was a camper, sort of. Except . . . no, not really. I'd actually been fighting hard against the whole idea of summer camp since the day Abby left, and even more since she'd tried to bring it back with her. I was a pillow forter, a builder of caves and doer of missions with the wind blowing through my hair. Abby was the one with the super-social summer camp skills, and meeting new people powers, and *oh my moose nostrils, that was it.*

Abby was the Camp. And I was the Pillow Fort. And we could only do this by our powers combined.

I turned my head. "Abby, get up here. I need you."

Abby looked surprised and more than a little wary, but she clambered to her feet and maneuvered her way beside me. "What are you doing?" she murmured, eyeing the sharp points of the antlers less than a foot above our heads.

"I think I figured it out," I said. "The moose helps campers, but I'm too much of a pillow forter to count. It should recognize you, though. What can you do that's Cantaloupey?"

"Huh? Cantaloupey?"

"You know, something from camp. Is there a song or— Hey! The camp dance!"

"What about it?" said Abby.

"It's perfect," I said. "Do it."

"Now?"

"Of course now! You were all about it the other day. And we need to do something to convince the moose we're campers worth saving. You do it once to show me, then I'll join in. I think we're supposed to do this thing together."

The moose was watching our discussion with interest.

Abby paused, and I bit my lip. I could almost hear Old Abby and New Abby fighting it out.

The thing was, I needed help from both.

"Oh-kay," she said at last. "Fine." I moved back, relieved, as she put her hands on her hips and stepped into a deep lunge. "But this had better work, or I'm gonna feel really silly. And one, two, three: da-da, da-da-da, da, DA . . ."

It wasn't a complicated dance, and Abby gave it her all even while wobbling on blankets and trying not to step on Uncle Joe. She kicked, lunged, swayed, and clapped, da-da-ing along the whole time.

"Okay," she said, coming to a halt. "That's the Camp Cantaloupe dance. Here, Mags." She held out a hand. "Let's try it with both of us."

Space was tight, so we wrapped our arms around each other's shoulders. It was nice being huddled up—it took the edge off the cold. We stepped into a deep lunge.

"You all might as well help too," called Abby, half turning around. "Like Maggie said, maybe we're supposed to do this together."

I glanced back. Matt, Mark, and my mom looked confused.

Kelly looked excited. Samson was asleep.

"We can do the singing part," announced Kelly, pushing away the blankets of her cocoon. "I like to sing. Okay, one, two, three . . . da-da, da-da-da, da, DA. . . ."

And Abby and I danced. It took a few tries to get in sync, but we got there in the end. One by one the others joined in on the da-da-ing, and soon Kelly was conducting with Creepy Frog, Mark was drumming with his wrench, and the bed of the truck was bouncing with our kicks and lunges.

I had a sudden vision of how weird all this would look to someone out there in the mists. A hodgepodge family of kids, teens, and grown-ups, camped out in a pickup truck, putting on a song-and-dance routine for a dinosaur-size moose in the middle of the freezing arctic night.

"Cantaloupes," I murmured to myself, squeezing Abby closer for the swaying bit. "We are a total bunch of cantaloupes." I grinned. I wasn't cold at all anymore.

Halfway through the fourth round the moose began to nod its huge nose up and down in time with our dancing.

"It's working!" panted Abby, and we danced even harder.

As the fifth round ended the moose let out a loud snort, reared up high, its hairy belly stretching over our heads, and brought its hooves back to earth with a crash. More rocks shattered. Abby and I froze midlunge, and the others stopped singing.

The moose snorted again, almost daintily in the silence,

then turned and trotted a few steps into the mist. It stopped and looked back, just visible in the reflection from the headlights, waiting.

"Well, that's pretty clear," said Abby, wiping her forehead on her sleeve. "Follow that moose!"

Kelly cheered. Matt and Mark whooped. Samson woke up and yawned.

Abby seized me and pulled me into a massive hug. She smelled like wool sweaters and cocoa and my best friend in the whole world. "Cantaloupe, cantaloupe," I said, grinning into her hair.

"Moose, moose, moose," she whispered back. "Thank you."

"Well done, Maggie and Abby!" called my mom, starting the engine with a roar as Abby and I flopped back in our seats. "Well done, everybody!"

The tires spun to life against the rocks and we were off, sliding through the fog with the moose trotting along between the headlights and everyone patting Abby and me on the back for being so brave. Everything was fun again, and the cold and damp and hunger were all just part of the adventure. Samson stretched out beside Uncle Joe—who had somehow slept through the whole entire thing—and purred even louder than the engine.

All at once the moose picked up speed and broke into a

run, disappearing in the clouds ahead. My mom stepped on the gas to follow, and as we zoomed forward, the mist around us thinned, faded, then vanished completely, and we were through. The dream was over, we were out of the valley, and spread out before us in the distance lay the roads and buildings and spangled lights of town.

TWENTY-THREE

Everything was quiet and still in the local hospital's pastel waiting room, and my head jerked up for the hundredth time as I fought to stay awake. Abby and Kelly were already asleep, curled up together on one of the couches with Samson hidden in a bundle of blankets between them. Matt and Mark slumped in their chairs, watching the silent TV on the wall and passing yawns back and forth. There was no one else around. Even the receptionist at the desk had gone for the night, and apart from Abby's snores it was perfectly still.

I was just giving in to the heavy pull behind my eyes when my mom arrived. I shook Abby and Kelly awake, and they sat up, yawning, crinkling the pile of wrappers from our Rescue Mission Snack Committee raid on the hospital vending machines.

"All right," my mom said, dropping into a chair. "Joe's going to be fine. It was a clean break, so no worries about long-term damage to his leg, and he's got a mild concussion, but they say that'll be fine too." She looked around at us, bleary-eyed and rumpled. "You're all real heroes."

"Did they ask who we were?" said Abby.

"Yes. I said we were tourists on a family trip."

"And they believed that?" I eyed my mom's purple scrubs and the oversize coats and sweaters the rest of us were wrapped in. We didn't exactly look like tourists.

"I think so," said my mom. "I told them we needed to do laundry and were down to our emergency backup outfits. Maybe they bought it, I don't know. Most doctors are used to seeing unusual things."

"This is the quietest hospital I've ever been in," said Kelly.

"I know—it's weird, isn't it?" said my mom. "But it's also the biggest one for miles. 'For half the size of Texas' one of the doctors told me, whatever that means. It's downright tiny compared to what I'm used to, but if they make Joe better, then it's the best hospital in the world."

"Did you tell them about the moose?" I asked. Before everyone quieted down we'd been debating whether our rescuer had been an actual ghost moose or just a friendly real one. Mark said it was probably a real one, since we'd been able to hear it walking on the rocks, and I'd had to admit I could smell it. But Abby kept pointing out how it had been there one minute and gone the next as soon as we reached town, and no one could come up with an answer for that.

My mom nodded. "I mentioned it, but the nurses insisted they don't have moose up here this time of year."

"Ha! See?" said Abby, waving Creepy Frog in triumph.

"Maybe they don't," said Kelly, "but we do." Abby high-fived her.

"What happens now?" asked Matt. "If Joe's gonna be okay, should we all just head home?"

"Definitely," said my mom. "I'm exhausted, and I don't even want to think what's going on back at *my* hospital. My shift was almost over when you came to get me, but Kelly's supposed to be in her room and we've been gone for hours and hours...."

"I locked the door and turned off the lights," I said. "We thought that might help."

"Yeah, I saw that when I went back for those pain meds for Joe. And it might, if I can convince my colleagues we were telling ghost stories or holding a séance or something." Kelly giggled. My mom ran a hand over her eyes. "But what I don't see is how we're going to get home anytime soon. Even with the sun coming up, it's a long drive back to the cabin."

"Dude! If only we had a token with us," said Abby, slapping the sofa. "There are plenty of pillows. We could have built a fort and linked straight home from here."

"Why didn't we think of that before?" I said. I was off my game. Keeping an emergency backup token around should have been obvious.

"Hey, so I'm not sure I get what you two are saying," said Mark, "but is there a chance you're wishing for something like this?" He dug around in his pocket and pulled out ... our map of Camp Pillow Fort.

Abby and I stared at him.

"What?!"

"Where did you get that?"

"I picked it up in Maggie's fort earlier," said Mark. "I thought a map might come in handy during a rescue mission."

"That is seriously good thinking!" said Abby. "All right, let's get to work."

We didn't need a fancy fort, and after a quick planning meeting run by Kelly, who was the only one with experience building forts in hospitals, we settled on a simple half circle of pillows around one of the sofas. Abby threw her blanket over the top, Matt placed the map inside, and just to be safe we all counted to ten.

"Is that it?" asked Matt.

"That's it," I said.

"You're not scared it might have accidentally linked to

a laser-eyed wild boar reserve or something, Mags?" asked Abby, elbowing me.

"Ha! You're funny." I elbowed her back. She was teasing, but it was nice to realize that I actually wasn't expecting things to go wrong here. For the first time in a while I was pretty certain everything was going to turn out all right.

"It should be good to go," I said. "Who's first?"

"Kelly first," said my mom. "Then me."

"Cool. Okay, Kelly, off you— Aaah!"

I wasn't the only one who yelled as a loud clamoring suddenly erupted inside the fort. It sounded like a roomful of people having an argument. One voice rose above the others.

"I'm dealing with it. I am *dealing* with it!"

We all jumped back as a sandy-haired kid wearing silver sunglasses materialized out of the brand-new entrance.

"What—!"

"How—?"

"Murray!?"

"Oh, it *is* you," said Murray, pushing his shoulders through the gap and propping himself up on his elbows. "It's wonderful to see you, Maggie, but honestly, would you please stop breaking every rule we have? Building new forts, adding links left and right, telling adults? I know you've declared an official emergency, but you are becoming a total menace."

My mouth was hanging open.

"But, but we only just built— How did you find—?"

"How did I find you?" Murray said. "I'm Captain of the Northern and Arctic Alliance! You're on my turf. And causing a lot of confusion among my membership, I might add. They think we're being invaded, eh?"

"Maggie," said my mom, "who is this boy? And why is he wearing sunglasses at night?"

"Um, everyone, this is Murray," I said. "He's head of the pillow fort networks for this area and on the Council of NAFAFA. They all wear silver sunglasses."

"What on earth is the Council of Nuh-foo-foo?" asked Matt.

"They're the ones who messed up our homes," said Abby. She was glaring at Murray. "They deliberately got us in trouble just because we weren't following the rules of their silly club."

I looked at Abby in surprise. She'd been all excited about joining NAFAFA before. Maybe those hours of backbreaking work in the rat-infested alley had changed her mind.

"Hey, hey, hey," said Murray. "There's no need to go insulting NAFAFA. You're talking about one of the most respected pillow fort organizations in the world."

"Really?" said Mark.

"It is actually pretty cool," I said, "and historical. Marilyn

Monroe and Aretha Franklin were members."

"Don't forget Alex Trebek," said Murray.

"He's Canadian, you know," I told the others.

"Neat," said Matt.

"This is the strangest conversation I've ever been a part of," said my mom.

Murray gave a sudden start. "Oop! Hang on, someone's got my foot." He disappeared into the fort, then stuck his head out again. "A friend wants to say hi, Maggie."

He retreated, and the head and shoulders of another boy appeared in the link.

"Hi! Maggie! Maggie-Maggie-Maggie!"

"Bobby," I said, grinning. "Good to see you."

"You too!" Bobby reached out and grasped my hands. "How have you been? Murray says you've been breaking rules and having adventures! Everyone's been talking about it."

"Really?"

"Really!" He smiled around at the others. "Hi, Maggie's people! I'm Bobby!" Everyone waved and said hi back. "You all know Maggie's a superstar, right?" he went on. "Because she is. She's brave and curious and wonderful, and you're so, *so* lucky to have her as your leader."

Abby made a high-pitched noise in her throat and gripped my arm. The others all turned to me, beaming. Bobby was still holding my hands. My face burned hotter than the roof tiles at noon.

"Everyone already knows that!" called a muffled voice from inside the makeshift fort. Abby made the noise again and squeezed my arm tighter as Murray pushed his way in beside Bobby. "I mean you do, right?" he asked, flashing his sunglasses at the group.

"Obviously," said Abby. The twins grinned. Kelly and my mom patted me on the back.

Oh, my woolly mammoth. I had to put a stop to this.

"What exactly do you want, Murray?" I said. "We're kind of in a hurry here."

"Ah! You're busy with business!" said Bobby, releasing my hands. "I'll get out of the way, then. I just *had* to come say hello. So Hello! And Good-bye! Good-bye, Maggie, and Maggie's people! See you all soon!" And blowing kisses to each of us in turn, he backed into the fort and disappeared.

There was an outbreak of giggling. I kept my focus on Murray, flatly refusing to catch Abby's eye.

"Okay, yes, business," Murray said. He cleared his throat. "Now that I've made sure it's you, the reason I'm here is to tell you that given the, well, *mess* you two have made of the NAFAFA application process, the Council has decided to cut your trial period short. Your time's up, and we're voting tomorrow. Or later today, I guess, if you want to get technical."

"What?!" Abby said.

"You can't do that!"

"I'm really sorry, Maggie," said Murray, and he looked like he meant it, "but we can. There's a lot going on with the Council right now, what with Noriko aging out next month, and to be honest, we just want this over."

"We're going to get in, though, right?" I said. "We rescued Uncle Joe! That should be more than enough."

"It should be," said Murray. "But we'll have to wait and see. If your official emergency really is finished, the best thing you can do now is get back where you belong and stay there."

Samson, who'd been sleeping through all the excitement in his bundle of blankets, sat up and yawned, stretching luxuriously. He hopped down, sauntered over to the fort, and sniffed Murray's face.

"Hello," said Murray. "You'll be the director of Camp Pillow Fort, eh? Do you have anything to say on behalf of your network?"

Samson head-butted Murray's chin and pushed past him into the fort.

"That means he likes you," said Abby.

"Sorry, did you say 'director'?" asked my mom.

"Samson's the director of our network," I said. "He won the vote."

"And that's causing all sorts of other problems," said Murray. "Ben keeps pointing out that according to the NAFAFA charter, Council seats *have* to be held by the highest-ranking member of each regional group, which means if you all get voted in the seat is technically Samson's. And that's just not going to work. Not only is Miesha super allergic to cats, but where exactly are we supposed to find sunglasses that would fit his little kitty face?"

That got a happy laugh from Kelly, but her laugh turned into a cough, and my mom instantly snapped into doctor mode.

"Okay, kids," she said, clapping her hands, "no more nonsense. I'm taking Kelly back to her room right now, and I mean now. Murphy, or whatever your name is, you do not want to be in my way here."

"Yes, ma'am," said Murray. "I've got places to be too." He lowered his sunglasses and looked at me. "Maggie, I don't know what's going to happen with the Council, but one way or another you'll hear from us sometime tomorrow morning, west coast time. For now, I'm counting on you to please get everyone back where they're supposed to be. And make sure you close this fort off after you."

"Got it."

"See you soon, I hope." Murray waved good-bye and started backing up, then stopped. He seemed to be struggling with himself. Before I could ask what was wrong, he raised a hand and blew a kiss right to me—and only me—turned fire engine red, and vanished into the fort.

Abby made the noise again.

One by one we headed back, first Kelly, then my mom, then Abby. I held out a hand for Matt to go ahead of me and got one of his dazzling smiles in return.

"Thanks for letting me tag along, Maggie," he said. "This was fun. Things are pretty awesome when you're in charge."

"Shmer, fenny lime!" I said casually. Matt winked and followed Abby, who was directing Mark back home.

I came through last with the map, pulling the pillow shut behind me and closing the door on a long and extremely weird day.

"I wonder what the doctors will think when they can't find us and there's just this random empty fort in the waiting room," I said.

Abby shrugged. "Probably the same thing they were thinking when we turned up: that we're one complete bunch of cantaloupes."

We were both tired beyond tired, so after helping me stuff all the blankets and jackets back through to Uncle Joe's, Abby headed off to bed. I climbed onto my sofa bunk, yawned, and took one last look around at Fort McForterson's quiet links. So much was about to change. Even if the Council voted us in, my mom was involved now, and Alex would probably find out soon too, and what would that mean for our secret club? And if the Council voted to shut us down, right when things were getting good, well ... we'd just have to cross that bridge when we came to it.

I yawned again, feeling like Samson, and finally, finally, finally drifted off to sleep.

TWENTY-FOUR

I woke up late the next morning, stumbled groggily into the kitchen, and found myself face-to-face with something I hadn't seen in years: my mom, wearing a bathrobe, cooking breakfast.

"Morning," she said, poking at the frying pan. "I took the day off."

I gaped at her. She might as well have told me she'd decided to become a moose.

Over a breakfast of lumpy pancakes, she filled me in on what happened when she and Kelly got back to the hospital the night before. Apparently Kelly had taken charge of the whole thing, telling the nurses how she and my mom had been reading the most *amazing* book about time-traveling cats and how it was so good she had absolutely positively *refused* to let my mom stop reading until it was over. Kelly had been extremely convincing, and everyone had decided my mom was a first-class physician for spending so much time with one patient, and somehow, miraculously, everything was okay.

We were sitting around the counter drinking orange juice and ignoring the dishes when there was a knock at the back door. It was Abby, looking happy, and Alex, carrying an enormous pan of cinnamon rolls.

"Morning," said Alex, setting the pan on the counter. "Sorry for just dropping by like this, Karen. I brought some treats."

"Hi, Alex," said my mom. "It's fine. And thank you!"

"Maggie," said Alex, "I was hoping to have a private talk with your mom. Would you and Abby mind giving us some space for a bit?"

I looked to my mom, who nodded, so Abby and I helped ourselves to cinnamon rolls and clambered up on the roof.

"So, what happened with your dad?" I asked, turning my back on the pine tree and diving into the frosting. Holy turtle poop, it was good. It was the greatest thing I'd had since guacamole lasagna.

"He was waiting up," said Abby. "I thought he would be really mad, but he said when he got back from his date and all of us were gone he knew we must be together, and that meant we were safe. He still wanted a complete explanation of where we'd been, though."

"Whoa! What did you tell him?"

"Everything. Well, the twins did. Matt explained how I couldn't say anything now that the emergency was over, not without getting us all in trouble with the Council, so they told him as much as they knew."

I wiped some frosting off my chin. "And did he believe them?"

"He went really quiet and sort of thought for a while, then he said he wanted to sleep on it. But this morning when I woke up he didn't even mention it. He just called me into the kitchen and asked if I wanted to help him try out this new cinnamon roll recipe he got from Tamal."

"I think I might be in love with Tamal," I said, shoving another piece of cinnamon roll into my mouth.

"Aww, poor Murray," Abby said.

I elbowed her in the ribs.

"So you're not in trouble with your dad anymore, then? Everything's all right?"

"Yup," said Abby. "While we were making the cinnamon rolls, he told me he'd rather believe his kids were telling the truth. And anyway, it was a great story and he really hoped it was true." She looked around. "Okay, I'm going to need a napkin here."

Alex came out the back door as we were climbing down off the roof.

"Have a good day, kids," he called. "Sounds like you'll be hanging out here for a while. Bring the pan back when you come home, okay, Abby?"

Abby gave a sticky thumbs-up. Back in the kitchen my mom was wolfing down a cinnamon roll of her own.

"Oh, my purple scrubs," she said with her mouth full. "These are incredible!"

"Right?" I said. "What did you and Alex talk about?"

She swallowed. "Mr. Hernandez wanted to check in with me about what happened last night. It sounds like he knew a bit already from the boys, but he still had a lot of questions."

"And you answered them?"

"I told him the truth, yes."

Ugh. The idea of our parents talking about the forts on their own made me incredibly nervous. They didn't know enough. What if they jumped to some weird, grown-up conclusions about what should happen next? What if they decided they should take the forts away from us? Or worse, what if they wanted to get involved?

"So . . . what do you think?" I asked, bracing for the worst.

"I think I really need this cinnamon roll recipe," said my mom, turning her attention back to her plate.

Abby looked over at the clock and nudged me. "When do

you think we'll hear from the Council? I wish they'd just let us know already and get it over with."

"I haven't checked my fort for messages since you got here," I said. "Maybe they already have."

But there were no silver envelopes or Council members waiting for us in Fort McForterson, just Samson stretched out in the link between our houses, purring like he didn't have a care in the world.

The phone in the kitchen blared. My mom answered it, and I heard her let out a whoop.

"Kids! Get in here—it's Joe!" We ran back to the kitchen as my mom put the phone on speaker.

Uncle Joe sounded great. He said the doctors up in Alaska were baffled by the disappearance of "that weird tourist family," but he was claiming ignorance across the board as a result of his concussion. He was already using his hospital time to sketch out a paper on Orpheus and his tremendous scientific discovery, and his doctors were already sick of hearing about it. At one point my mom tried to explain why and how we'd left him all alone at the hospital, but Uncle Joe stubbornly la-la-ed over her until she stopped, and she had to let it go.

By the time we hung up the phone Abby and I were feeling pretty good about everything, even if the Council was taking forever to vote. My mom, however, turned out to have a bone to pick with us.

"Okay, you two," she said, leaning against the counter and folding her arms. "Now that we know everyone is okay, I'm sorry to say, this is where I step in." Abby shot me a glance. "I want to acknowledge that what you two have discovered is extraordinary, in the literal sense of the word, but here's the thing, and Mr. Hernandez agrees with me on this: Now that I know, I can't—as a parent, doctor, grown-up, any of it—let you keep having free access to your forts, even if those Council kids decide to let you join their club."

Our jaws crashed right through the floor.

"It's a question of safety and responsibility," said my mom, ignoring our stunned faces. "Not to mention academics. You're starting middle school in the fall, and you'll need to focus on work, not running in and out of each other's houses at all hours of the day and night, which"—she raised a hand as I tried to interrupt—"I know you've been doing, so it's no use arguing."

"How do you know?" I demanded.

"Because that's exactly what I would have done at your age," said my mom. "A magical pillow fort kingdom with my best friend? I would have gotten into so much trouble."

"But we haven't gotten into any trouble," said Abby. "At least not because of things we've actually done."

"And that's the way I want to keep it," said my mom, nodding. "Besides, think about the stuff you have gotten up to, in just a few days. Sneaking around people's homes at night?

.aking food without permission? Fibbing to your parents about where you are? It sounds like harmless kid stuff, and maybe it is, but those are some seriously blurry lines there, and chances are one day you're going to cross a real one.

"And what about Alaska? What if one of you got badly hurt on one of your trips? Or separated from the others and lost? I don't think you understand how lucky you've been so far. I'd never stop worrying about you if I let this continue, and I'm sorry, but the fact is it's not safe and it's got to stop."

"But this is ours," said Abby. "We created Camp Pillow Fort by ourselves. You can't just make us shut it down!"

"I can't let you continue to run wild either, Abby," said my mom. "So what I'm proposing is a compromise. You can keep using the forts, and the links, and all the rest of it, but only with me as chaperone. Or camp counselor, if you prefer that term."

We stared at her in dead silence. I could hear the kitchen clock ticking.

"Oh, come on, you don't have to look so defeated," said my mom, smiling. "I can't go with you everywhere—I'll be at work too much. But I will need to know which fort you'll be in, when, and for how long, and approve any and all trips to Alaska ahead of time. And any new *links*, I think you called them, will have to be coordinated with the permission of parents on both sides. But that's it. Apart from that I'll only interfere if things are getting out of hand."

I looked over at Abby. Abby looked over at me. We were agreed: no way. It was impossible. My mom might as well have asked us to take the forts down then and there.

"What about Kelly?" I asked, putting off having to give an answer. "That wasn't 'running wild.' We did a really nice thing for her."

"That's actually even more serious," said my mom. "I saw her fort, so I know you did a nice thing for her, but what you may not know is that it's incredibly unsafe bringing knick-knacks into a hospital like that. It wasn't just decorations, it was germs and allergens, too. Kelly will be fine—she's actually getting better—but I work with some very sick kids, and you could have done one of them real harm. So Kelly's fort is going to have to be closed off. Period. I know she'd love to have you come visit her the normal way while she's still in the hospital, but the health and safety of my patients is more important than anything else."

We hung our heads. That was bad. We never meant to put anyone in danger.

"Now, don't worry," said my mom. "Everything turned out okay." She smiled encouragingly. "And it's not like the adventure's ending, is it? You'll just be getting a brand-new member."

She actually seemed excited at the idea of joining in. I

.lmost felt sorry about breaking the bad news.

"Well, see, the thing is, even if the Council votes us in, grown-ups aren't—"

But I never got to finish telling her, because a scuffling suddenly erupted from the living room. Abby and I jumped up just in time to see the front of Fort McForterson fly open and a kid in silver sunglasses crawl out. It was Miesha.

I grabbed Abby's arm. Finally, this was it!

Miesha got to her feet, spotted us, raced into the kitchen . . . and shoved the key from le Petit Salon into my hands.

TWENTY-FIVE

"Here!" said Miesha. "Take this. Keep it safe." She had feathers stuck to her shirt and pillow stuffing in her hair.

"What is— Why are—" I said. "What happened to you?"

"Anyone can see I just won a pillow fight," said Miesha, fishing a feather from between her fancy tortoishell and silver Council glasses.

"How do you win a pillow fight?" asked Abby.

"By being in one."

"Oh." Abby smiled. "Well, don't keep us waiting! How did the vote go?"

"The vote hasn't happened yet," said Miesha, backing up toward the living room. "We've been too busy with other things. Just keep that key safe." She sneezed violently. A handful of feathers floated to the ground. "Ugh, I passed your cat coming through your fort. Allergies are the worst."

"But, wait, you haven't voted?" I held up the key. "What's this for, then?"

Miesha stopped and glanced at the clock on the stove. "Oh, all right. I can spare a couple minutes to explain."

"Sweet!" Abby patted a stool. "In that case, you have to, have to, have to try one of these cinnamon rolls."

"Ooh, thanks!"

We all sat down as my mom plated up a roll. Miesha dove right in. "Okay, wow! This is incredible! Way to go, local Snack Committee. But yes, news, super important." She swallowed and took a deep breath. "So, last night one of Ben's clipboard spies found out Noriko set up that alley-cleaning deed for you. Big drama. Ben made a formal protest and called to have the Council remove her from power."

"Isn't he's always doing that?" I said.

"Yes," said Miesha around another bite of cinnamon roll. "But this time he told his whole network about it first, and they all turned up to support him. Things got, you know, heated, and soon everyone was involved, and I mean *everyone*. There were snacks flying everywhere and pillow fights in every corner of the Hub. NAFAFA hasn't been through something like this since the Great Stuffed Animal Debate of 2009. Anyway, in the end Noriko had to step down as leader just to ease the tension."

"What?!" said Abby. "You mean you gave in?"

"Calm down," said Miesha. "Calm down, it was her idea. Well, hers and mine. Noriko's aging out of NAFAFA so soon it doesn't really matter to her. And she's still on the Council for now—she's just not head anymore."

"Who is, then?" I demanded.

"No one. We're on a cooling-off break before we vote on who the next leader will be. After *that* we can decide whether you all should get in. Like I told you, we've got a lot going on."

"Wow," I said. It was weird to think all that had been happening while I'd been sound asleep in my fort. "But wait." I spotted a major problem here. "Wasn't the whole point to get us on the Council before Noriko stepped down so we could be the fourth vote for you? Isn't having no leader exactly what Ben wanted? Won't he hold his vote hostage until he gets our territory?"

Miesha sneezed. "Ugh, sorry," she said. "And you're absolutely right, Maggie Hetzger. That's where my part of the plan comes in. Noriko stepping down has Ben *thinking* he's already won. But he doesn't know you have that key—my idea, thank you, thank you—and once he realizes you do, we can put as much pressure on him as it takes to get me elected head."

"This. Is. Incredible," said Abby, staring wide-eyed at Miesha. She was completely entranced. "Intrigue! But, okay, why does us having this key let us tell Ben what to do?"

"Because Ben's obsessed with that key," I said. "He thinks he's the chosen one or whatever, and that someday it'll let him open the door in le Petit Salon."

"Exactly," said Miesha. "With you holding it hostage here, I've got him by the overalls. Either he gives up the west coast for good, votes for me as head, then votes you in along with the rest of us, or we cut you two off permanently from all links and he never sees it again. He'll have to do what we tell him. He's got no choice." She took another bite. "Mmph, seriously, why don't I eat cinnamon rolls every day?"

"That is brilliant!" Abby said. "Is there anything we can do to help?"

Miesha snort-laughed just like Abby. "Aw, thanks," she said bopping her with an elbow, "but this is already way outside your skill set. I want you on my Council, for sure, but you two are still beginners here, and I've been doing this stuff for years. Just hang on to that key, keep it safe, and I'll come get you after it's all over. I'm totally making you two in charge of Snack Committee once I'm head, by the way. You bring these to every Council meeting and we'll probably never have a serious pillow fight again!"

She beamed at me. I smiled back as best I could, but my brain was spinning.

I honestly didn't know what to think anymore. Was being

on the Council always going to be like this? This constant battle of votes and plans and hostages and schemes? It wasn't exactly the type of secret-agent detective work I'd signed up for. And how could Miesha say she wanted us on her side, then calmly talk about shutting us down for good if she and the others didn't get their way?

"Wow, that sure is a lot to take in," said my mom. I jumped. I'd completely forgotten she was in the room.

Miesha nodded. "Yes, ma'am, it is. And like I said, that's why you all should just leave it to the pros." She glanced at the stove clock. "Thanks again for the amazing cinnamon roll, but I really gotta get back. Don't worry—one of us will be in touch soon."

We said good-bye and watched her disappear into Fort McForterson. My head was pounding with questions, questions, and more questions, but it looked like I'd have to wait until after the vote to get any answers.

I was about to ask Abby what she wanted to do while we waited when there was a cry from the fort, followed by a yowl and a storm of angry hissing.

"Samson!" cried Abby. We jumped up and ran for the living room.

"Hey, you've got a rat in here!" came Miesha's yell. "Also—*achoo!*—angry—cat! Great."

Abby reached the quaking fort first and ducked inside.

"Oh!" she said. "It's Mr. Chompers!"

I followed after her and stopped in the entrance, staring.

The fort was in pandemonium. Half the links were knocked open, postcards were flying everywhere, and the contents of my arts-and-crafts corner were scattered wildly across the floor.

Abby had become a one-girl hurricane flailing after Samson, who was tearing around and around in circles, hot on the heels of an enormous, panicked rat. Miesha was up against the sofa in a standing crouch, sneezing nonstop and dancing from foot to foot, trying to reach her link without stepping on anyone. As I watched, Samson and the rat streaked right between her feet and she staggered, slipped on Creepy Frog, and fell hard, grabbing at the walls on the way down. The ceiling began to collapse.

"Gotcha!" cried Abby, seizing Samson around the middle. "Are you okay, Miesha? Ouch, Samson! Maggie, get that ceiling up!"

"On it!" I said, shoving the key in my pocket and squeezing in to help.

It was chaos. I battled against the blanket and fallen pillows; Abby wrestled with a squirming Samson; Miesha sneezed nonstop and clawed her way toward the link to the Hub; and the huge rat tore over everything—pillows, books, and people—in a scrabbling panic.

I struggled to my feet just in time to see Mr. Chompers make a sharp turn, scamper up one of Miesha's legs, and disappear through the half-open link back to the alley. Miesha spun around, kicking frantically at the tumbled pillows.

"It's out," I said, batting at the collapsing ceiling sheet with my arms. "The rat's out! Quick, close the link!"

"Kinda busy here," said Abby. "Samson, let go!"

"Ugh, rats!" said Miesha. *"Achoo!"* She scrambled away on her hands and knees, making a beeline for her link. "Only thing worse—*achoo!*—than cats!"

"Mags, grab that alley pillow."

"I'm holding the ceiling up!"

"Achoo!"

"Miesha, wait, you've got my scarf—"

"Ouch! There, you're back home, Samson."

"Miesha, stop!" I yelled.

Abby looked up at the panic in my voice and spotted what had made my blood go cold: my patchwork scarf was wrapped around Miesha's right ankle.

"Nope, you've got your—*achoo!*—instructions!" Miesha crawled faster, her head and shoulders already back through the link. "I've had—*achoo!*—enough of this—*achoo!*—zoo. This is like being in the worst—*achoo!*— Lisa Frank—*achoo!*— picture ever!"

"Miesha!" Abby yelled as I threw myself across the fort,

reaching desperately—but it was too late. Miesha's feet slipped neatly into the NAFAFA Hub, and the colorful tangle of my patchwork scarf went with her.

A gentle breeze swept through the fort as all the links snapped shut, and the ceiling settled over us like a soft and terrible cloud.

TWENTY-SIX

It was Abby who finally pulled the sheet away. My mom stood in the kitchen doorway with her arms crossed, watching.

"Is that it, then?" she asked as we emerged.

Abby nodded.

"No more magic pillow forts?"

I shook my head.

"Oh, I'm so sorry, kids." She watched us for another moment, then slipped quietly down the hall.

We sat together in the ruins of Fort McForterson, grieving and silent, until Abby clambered to her feet and reached out a hand. She had some impressive new scratches on her forearms, and her fancy braid was coming undone. I let her pull me up.

"So, they took away my scarf after all," I said. "We're back where we started."

"Yup," said Abby. She sighed. "But hey, at least we had some adventures in the real world for once."

I gave a half smile. "Eh. It could've been better. More chase scenes. And a volcano would have been nice. And would it kill us to finally get to ride in a helicopter?"

Abby forced a laugh. "Oh, hey," she said, bending down and pulling something out of the remains of the fort. She handed it to me. It was Miesha's silver sunglasses.

"Huh, it must have been all the sneezing," I said. "Hope she's got a spare pair. Do you want them?"

"Nope."

"Same." I turned them over in my hand. They didn't mean much now that we'd never get to be on the Council. I looked around, then leaned down and put them on Creepy Frog.

"Ha," said Abby. She gazed at the fort, stirring the mess of fallen blankets with her foot. "Why did you call it Gromit's Room, again?" she asked.

I looked at her. "Seriously? Welcome home, finally." Abby had the grace to look a little embarrassed.

It was weird. With the loss of Fort McForterson, I'd gotten everything I'd spent the summer wishing for: my best friend all to myself, with no one around who might take her away from me. Only I wasn't feeling even the teeniest bit happy. We'd lost our whole glorious, tangled, oddball new world just as I'd been getting the hang of it. And with our only scrap of First Sofa trapped somewhere we could only reach with a working link, there really was no way back.

"I can't believe those Council kids are making everything so messy and complicated," said Abby. "We'd do such a better job if we were the ones in charge."

"Obviously," I said.

She grinned. "Hey, can I see this super-mysterious key?"

I pulled it out. The metal gleamed in the late-morning light, the oak leaves curling around the sun shining in the center.

"So this," said Abby, taking it and weighing it in her palm, "this is from France?"

"From le Petit Salon in the palace of Versailles. Yes."

It was a strange thing to hear myself say, standing there with Abby in my quiet Seattle living room.

"But it doesn't work in the door there?"

"Right. No one knows what lock it really goes to. Or why Louis hung on to it. It's been a mystery for centuries."

Abby held the key up to her nose. "This is a big deal, isn't it?" she said. "I mean, didn't you say—" She stopped and narrowed her eyes, squinting. Her hand shot out and whapped my arm. I yelped.

"Ouch! Dude, what—? Again with the hitting!"

"Mags! Mags-Mags-Mags-Mags!" she said, batting me on the shoulder. "Remember the tree house, the one at Camp

Cantaloupe I told you about? Made of driftwood and stuff that washed up onshore?"

"Vaguely," I said. "What—"

"Remember how I said it had a trapdoor, but it didn't open? The trapdoor was a solid piece of wood, an old one, with these metal bands across it, and a big heavy lock holding it shut. . . ."

"And?"

"And the lock was decorated with a sun surrounded by oak leaves."

Abby held out the key. I looked at it. I shook my head. "No. No way. That is too much of a coincidence. It's probably just similar."

Abby's eyes were as wide as moose nostrils. "I spent a lot of time trying to pick that lock, Mags. This key . . . it's identical."

My heart began to race as bits and pieces from the last few wild days whirled through my mind, stories and phrases reshaping themselves into brand-new patterns and puzzles. The storm on Orcas Island. The shipwreck tree house. The unknown ambassador. The sun-carved lock.

"So . . . ," I said, my stomach doing a series of giddy back-flips. "So, what do we think might happen if you and I go to Camp Cantaloupe, open that lock, and climb through the trapdoor of the tree house?"

Abby handed me the key and looped her arm through mine. "Only one way to find out, isn't there?" she said, and she marched me down the hall and knocked on my mom's bedroom door.

My mom appeared, carrying an armful of tangled sheets and towels. Abby grabbed my hand.

"Hey, Ms. Hetzger," she said. "Sorry to bother you, but here's the thing: since the forts are gone and nothing mysterious or magical is going on anymore, I just want to make absolutely, seriously, *definitely* sure that Maggie will be coming with me to Camp Cantaloupe next summer. No matter what."

My mom narrowed her eyes, giving the two of us a long, long look. Finally, she smiled.

"Right," she said, tossing the laundry pile to one side. "I'd better get a start on that paperwork, then."

ACKNOWLEDGMENTS

A first book has a whole lifetime of thanks behind it, so maybe get yourself some delicious lasagna or a cinnamon roll or something before you settle in here, dear reader.

First, enormous thanks to my mom, Cynthia St. Clair, for always keeping a dictionary by the dinner table and handing *The Dark is Rising* to this boy named Will when he turned eleven. To my dad, Ian Taylor, for introducing me to Ursula K. Le Guin and reading *The Lord of the Rings* to me by candlelight when I was small. And to my sister, Megan Taylor, for letting me borrow her Debbie Gibson tapes and *Sweet Valley High* books, cheering me on at every turn, and constantly inspiring me to be better than I am today.

All the brightest thanks to my wonderful agent, Emily Keyes, for taking a chance on an overeager hopeful and believing in this book when it wasn't there yet, and to everyone at Fuse Literary for giving me a home. Thank you to my entire team at HarperCollins: Jen Klonsky, Megan Barlog, Laura Kaplan, Renée Cafiero, Jessie Gang, and especially the brilliant Monique Dong for the swoon-worthy cover. And a thousand thank-you hugs to Elizabeth Lynch, the editor of my absolute dreams, who believed in Maggie and Abby right from the start and didn't laugh too hard when I couldn't figure out how to work the doors at the HarperCollins offices.

Deciding you want to be an author and starting to feel like one can be two very different things, and early kindness from Kevin O'Brien, Sarah Davies, Brent Taylor, and Jessica Sinsheimer helped me make that leap. Thank you all forever. And David Levithan, thank you for your unequaled support and encouragement, and for singing the high part of that George Michael–Elton John duet while we drove to Books of Wonder on a Sunday in the rain.

Enormous thanks to my Fran's Chocolates family for putting up with me while I went from planning to pitching to print, especially Anibel America, Sophie Froyland, Beyana Magoon, Maddy Bassett, and Marie Umetsu, who all had to listen to me babble about forts and links and synonyms for "pillow" for actual years.

Thanks and cheers to my old Seattle writing crew: Danielle Dreger, Megan Chodora, and Alex Kahler. Those chairs were so uncomfortable. I feel like we deserve nachos.

Extra-special thanks to Bethany C. Morrow and Marie Umetsu.

Massive thanks to my writing teachers over the years: Greta Gaard, Mary Cornish, Leanne Banton, Andy Barker, and above all Karen Mikolasy, the teacher who changed my life, pushed me more than I wanted to be pushed, and insisted that if I thought I was good at something, it just meant I had to work harder. I resented it then, but I can't stop thanking you for it now.

Special thanks to Rachel Marshall for not running away in terror when I turned up at your store with a book I'd written for you. Your self-control and ability to keep a straight face while you looked over my weirdly formatted, spiral-bound, middle grade pirate-adventure tribute to your ginger beer business was truly extraordinary.

Heartfelt thanks to Kate Bush. In general. Most of this book was written with you singing in the background, and if I pull off anything in this life, it's because you showed me it was possible to be impossibly romantic and ferociously independent at the exact same time.

A lifetime of thanks to my dear ones: Lindsey Newman and Amber Casali. You two have carried me through so, so much. The three of us have been linked since forever, no matter how far away our pillow forts get, and you are and always will be my family.

And finally, a truly neverending thank-you to Alex Kahler. This book absolutely would not exist without your support, kindness, and patience. You will always be the deep-magic winter raven to my sparkle-maned unicorn, and I can't wait to see what epic adventures we get up to next. By our powers combined, buddy.